The Abersoch

Adventure

By Steven McClernon

Prologue

The two men crouched behind a bush in the grounds of Grove house ensuring they were concealed from view. One glanced at his wristwatch; it was 1:30 a.m. The fog from the sea had rolled in towards the house giving the men the perfect cover, visibility was down to only a few metres in front of them. They stayed silent, listening and watching the big house, checking for any sound or movement from within, it was eerily dark and quiet. They had been observing the house the previous day, hidden in a nearby field which overlooked it. Through binoculars they had been checking to see how many people worked at the mansion but more importantly who stayed behind to retire to the servant's quarters at the rear of the great house. The two men had done this type of surveillance on four other country houses they had already burgled in the last few weeks.

"I think the coast is clear for us now mate" whispered one man to the other. They knew they could break in and not be disturbed as all the servants were sleeping at the rear of the property, and even if they did get caught they had a variety of weapons including pistols, just in case they had to overpower some doddering old games keeper with a shot gun! The more houses they robbed, the cockier they became. Almost thinking they were unstoppable, invincible!
They crept up to the front of the house, pulling their balaclava's down over their faces as they went. One of the men kept a look out; while the other pulled a crowbar from his holdall and started to force open the dining room window. It wasn't long before the lock gave way and broke, letting the man slide the window open and climb inside. A minute went by before he re-appeared at the open window and with a wave of his hand beckoned his accomplice inside too, as the coast was clear. Once inside each man knew his job

without needing to discuss it. They had sat down that afternoon and gone through the plan thoroughly, until they were both happy they knew their roles on the night. If they needed to communicate it was hand signals and whispering. One would search the room with his torch and fill a sack with silver and other valuables, while the other kept a look out at the door.

Once they were satisfied they had what they wanted, the sack was placed outside of the window they came in through. Then they both crept slowly into the dark hallway, making sure each placed foot step wasn't on a creaking floorboard. With the help from the beams of their torch lights they found the next room to ransack. As in the other houses they burgled, they would only stick to the downstairs rooms so they could quickly escape if they were disturbed. Also they would only take a maximum of two sacks of 'booty' each, so they weren't overloaded and could still move quickly when getting away. The criminals knew that these seaside mansions were owned by wealthy people with lavish lifestyles. They were the type of people who loved to entertain and throw big parties and liked to show off their valuable paintings and silverware. As they only came to their holiday homes for a few weeks of the year, it gave plenty of opportunities to be burgled.

Once they had filled the last of the sacks, they quietly carried them down the dark hallway and back into the dining room, closing the door behind them. A chair was then placed up against the door, wedged under the door handle as a means of slowing anyone down should they be heard and try to intervene.

One of the men climbed out of the open window and the other passed the remaining sacks out to him. He then climbed out himself and gently slid the window shut. He turned to his accomplice and smiled, then in a low voice said "house number five successfully robbed. We're getting good at this!" the other nodded and sniggered in agreement. The burglars knew that it would be later that morning before the staff of the house realised they had been broken into. By which time the men would be back at their hideout, celebrating their successful nights work and inspecting what valuables they had managed to acquire.

They checked all the sacks were securely tied shut, then picked up two each and headed off over the nearby fields from where they came and into the silent foggy night.

Chapter 1

It was a lovely warm sunny August day, Thomas and Catherine we're being dropped off at London Euston train station by their parents. It had taken what seemed like ages to drive from their home into central London. It was teaming with people trying to make their way to work, either on foot, in their cars or on one of the many red double decker buses.

The children's dad had to concentrate as he drove the family car. He weaved from lane to lane and checked road signs, making sure they didn't get lost.

Thomas was the youngest of the siblings at ten years old. He was medium height for his age with brown hair and brown eyes. His knees always seemed to be full of cuts and bruises due to him being quite clumsy. Catherine was the older sister, twelve years of age. She was quite a bit taller than her brother; she took after her dad who was tall himself. She had brown hair and green eyes. She was by no means a tomboy but she could look after herself if she needed to.

Thomas held his mum's hand tightly and Catherine her dad's as they snaked their way through the busy train station concourse. Everyone seemed to be in a rush, Commuters and holiday makers nearly bumping into one another as they raced to their waiting trains. Thomas looked up and could see the sunlight piercing through sections of the stations glass roof making it feel like they were in a greenhouse. Beams of light like giant pillars stretched from floor to ceiling. Within these giant pillars of light Thomas could see dust swirling around as people unknowingly passed through them. The children were making their way to the platform as they heard a man announce over the tannoy system that the train to Pwllheli had just arrived at Platform 2 and would depart at 09:16.

They were off to spend their summer holidays with their Aunt May in a place called Abersoch. Abersoch was a picturesque fishing village on the coast of North Wales. Thomas and Catherine had spent the last three summer holidays there whilst their mum and dad, both doctors, travelled abroad to work in an African missionary for the Red Cross charity. The children were so excited about returning to Abersoch, the countdown had started two weeks earlier. Each morning before breakfast they would race to the calendar and cross that day off, then count how many days were left until the big day. This was coloured in and had stars all around it!

Aunt May was their dad's older sister, in her late fifties she was a lovely woman, tall and thin with greying hair, but always well dressed and elegant. She was a widower, having lost her husband, their Uncle John, in World War Two. She had no children of her own and didn't particularly care for pets, 'she was too busy for all that nonsense!' as she put it. So she lived in Ashbourne house in Abersoch all alone, well apart from her staff. There was Charles the butler/chauffeur, Victoria the house keeper/maid, Sylvia the cook and Albert the gardener. Aunt

May had married into money as Uncle John's family were wealthy farmers and land owners. She spent most of her time socialising with her circle of friends, having coffee and book reading mornings, or organising local fairs and summer fates for Abersoch village.

Ashbourne house was on the edge of Abersoch; it had been in their Uncle John's family for generations and had been eventually passed down to him. A magnificent stone built Victorian style mansion within its own vast grounds. It had some seven bedrooms and numerous other rooms that Thomas and Catherine always loved to explore and have adventures in, especially on rainy days! To the rear of the house were rolling fields as far as the eye could see. The front of the house looked out onto the Abersoch coast, on a clear day the lighthouse at Warren Point could be clearly seen. At night its bright light beamed out to sea, warning passing ships of the jagged rocks of the peninsula.

Ashbourne house was a handful to keep tidy and in order, but Charles and Victoria ran it with military precision. Charles was a kind old man, very smart and proper but incredibly strict. 'There are rules and regulations in this house; it would help if you abide by them!' is what he would always say. It always brought a snigger from Thomas and Catherine, as it reminded them of an old school headmaster. They wondered if he had a cane to punish the rest of the servants with if they were naughty!

The children's parents helped them and their luggage into the train carriage. Their mum gave them both a big hug and a kiss, and then she started to cry. "I'm going to really miss you both, please be good for your aunt and most of all be careful, and look after one another". She always got upset when she had to leave them for more than a day. It was the same when they both had their first day at school; each time she got so upset she soaked her handkerchief with her tears!

Their dad hugged them both too "Have a wonderful time in Abersoch you two; you're so lucky to be spending you're summer holidays there. I wish I was coming instead of having to work! Right, well, we will see you in six weeks. When we're back from Africa, we will come and pick you up from Aunt May's". With that their parents got off the train and closed the carriage door, just in time as the train platform manager blew his whistle and waved his green flag to inform the train driver it was time to depart. The train began to shudder and creak then slowly move off, Thomas and Catherine stood at the open carriage window and waved at their parents on the platform who in turn were waving back. "I love you both, please be careful!" shouted their mum. "We will mum, we love you too" replied the children. The train now began to pick up speed and the train driver sounded the horn with a loud shriek. Then the steam and smoke covered the platform and their mum and dad disappeared out of site, Catherine pulled up the carriage window and sat down as did Thomas and they both settled into their journey to Pwllheli.

Chapter 2

The steam train chugged along the track, making its way across the country towards Wales. Thomas and Catherine passed the time by reading comics, eating lunch, watching the world go by through the carriage window, and finally snoozing. The journey seemed to take forever, but eventually they started to snake through the Snowdonia mountain range and knew they didn't have much further to travel. They had climbed up Snowdonia the year before when their parents had come for the last week of their summer holidays. Aunt May had lent them the Bentley and they drove to the mountain and spent the day climbing the great beast. They only got about half way as the weather took a change for the worse as it often did, and they were forced to turn around and come down.

Once through the mountains the land started to level out and the children kept getting glimpses of the sea, they could feel the train slowing down as it made its way to the final destination of Pwllheli train station.

Pwllheli was the main market town in the area; it was just down the coast from Abersoch. All the surrounding villages would bring their produce to sell at the local market twice a week. It also had the main fish market at the nearby marina as well. All the local fishermen would sell their catch here to local restaurants, fish and chip shops and the general public.

Pwllheli (pronounced Pwll-hell-ee) means 'salt water pool' in welsh. It had become popular with holiday makers over the years due to the Butlin's holiday camp just down the road.

The train's conductor came around and helped take Thomas and Catherine's heavy suitcases off the train for them and set them down onto the platform. They went and waited on a nearby bench and looked out for their expected familiar face. All their parents had told them was that Aunt May would send Charles to come and pick them up. Charles wasn't only the butler but doubled up as the chauffeur, taking Aunt May to all her social events and running any errands to the village. On this particular day he had been sent to Pwllheli train station to pick up the children and bring them back to Abersoch and Ashbourne house.

They finally saw the silhouette of a figure walking briskly almost marching, out through the train smoke towards them. It was Charles, by their standards a giant of a man at six feet tall. He was in his early fifties, of slim build with a long looking face, a greying moustache and short tidy black hair which was also starting to grey at the sides. He was very smartly dressed in his black butler's suit, white shirt and black tie, not forgetting his black trilby hat.
"Good afternoon children, I hope your journey was enjoyable, now we are on a tight schedule as your aunt is expecting you. So if you let me take your suitcases and kindly follow me, I have the car waiting outside the front of the train station" he said. Before the children had chance to reply,

Charles had picked up their suitcases, spun around on his heels and was heading back through the train smoke and to the exit.

Aunt May's car was parked outside the train station entrance. A shiny black 1930's Bentley. It was Uncle John's pride and joy. He loved to take it for a 'good thrashing' as he called it, around the nearby country roads. In its day it would have been one of the fastest cars on the road, even now it still made heads turn and look whenever it passed by. As it was her late husband's most prized possession, Aunt May could never part with it and always made sure it was kept in pristine condition. Thomas always got excited when he saw it and always wanted to travel in the front with Charles. Catherine on the other hand always travelled in the back and pretended she was a princess, being taken to her castle!

The drive from Pwllheli to Abersoch took them along the coast road. The children could see a few fishing boats bobbing up and down in

Cardigan Bay checking their crab pots for a catch. They drove through Llanbedrog village and passed the Glyn ye Weddow Arms pub. This was where some of the crabs would end up, on a 'Catch of the day' platter for the local holiday makers that venture in for lunch after a hard day on the nearby beach!

It didn't take long before they were turning into the grounds of Ashbourne house, past the large stone pillars with iron gates hanging from them and up the long sweeping driveway to the house. As Charles parked outside the main doors, Victoria the house keeper came running out to meet them as they were getting out of the car. She hugged them both tightly, "Master Thomas, Miss Catherine, oh how good it is to see you both. We've all been so excited, we're so glad you're finally here. I only said to Charles that it seems like yesterday you were on your last summer holidays ".

Charles just rolled his eyes and signed, "Alright Victoria now that's enough excitement for now let the children go and see their Aunt". With that he turned to get their suitcases out of the boot of the car.

Victoria looked at the children and in a lowered voice said "I've got your rooms ready for you just as you like them". Then she leant towards Catherine and whispered "Don't tell the gardener but I've picked some lovely flowers for you and put them in a vase in your room. I know how much you like them". Then she stood up and addressed them both again "Your Aunt is in the living room with her reading club, please go on in". Thomas and Catherine thanked Victoria and ran up the stone steps, through the large double oak doors into the house. They arrived at the living room door and Catherine knocked politely and waited, "come in" said their Aunt. The children went in, Aunt May was sat in a big red leather chair, book in hand. She looked up and saw the children running towards her; she dropped her book and lent forward to hug them. "Thomas, Catherine, oh it's good to finally see you". She then leant back in to her leather chair and examined them both carefully.

"Let me have a good look at you. Well it looks like your mother and father are feeding you well as you have both grown since the last time I saw you. Ladies, ladies for those of you who don't know my niece and nephew, let me introduce you to Thomas and Catherine. They have travelled up from London to spend the holidays here". All Aunt Mays friends said hello and Thomas and Catherine politely replied.

"Now you two run along, Albert has been dying to see you again; he hasn't stopped talking about you two since he found out you were coming. No doubt he'll be in that shed of his having his lunch. I will see you both later for supper" she said.
With that Thomas and Catherine left the living room and headed out into the large garden and across the vegetable patch to Albert's shed.
Catherine turned to Thomas, "I wonder what stories Albert's got for us this year Tom".
"Hope it's some good ones" he replied.

When they arrived at Albert's shed, the door was open a jar so they went racing in.

"Albert, Albert" they both shouted. Unfortunately for Albert, he'd just had lunch and was having an afternoon nap or 'forty winks' as he liked to call it, in his favourite old comfy armchair. Startled he jumped up with a 'Yelp',
"Goodness you two, you nearly gave me a heart attack!" Once he got his breath back, he knelt down and hugged them both. "It's great to see you both, hope you haven't missed me to much?" then he laughed.
"Hope you've got some good gossip for us Albert" said Thomas.
"Well as it happens I have. Everyone in Abersoch is really worried at the moment. Here pull up a couple of crates, I'll get the kettle on, then tell you all about it".

Chapter 3

Albert told Thomas and Catherine all about the burglaries over the past few weeks. He was like the local news reporter; he knew everyone and seemed to get to know all the gossip going. Like when Henry Donaldson's dog got its head stuck in the local park railings and Bob the Mechanic had to use his crowbar and some grease to free him. Albert seemed to be the one with the breaking news, telling everyone the details even though he was never there!

"Old Constable Finney is overwhelmed with all these burglaries. Nothing this big has happened around here before, he's used to giving kids a clip around the ear for trying to pinch sweets from the local newsagents; or making sure the drunks don't cause any bother at pub closing time". The man Albert was referring to was Constable William Finney, a tall thin man in his early Fifties, with black rimmed spectacles, a bushy greying moustache and short grey hair. He was un-married and lived alone above the police station but had a tabby cat called Stanley to keep him company. He had been the local policeman in Abersoch for the past fifteen years, but was hoping to eventually pass the reins over to a younger constable. The young man in question was Constable Jones still in training and being mentored by Constable Finney. He helped man the station and sort out the admin.

The police station had been in-undated with locals claiming to have seen shady characters lurking around here and there, busy bodies telling Constable Finney who he should arrest and question. He was using Constable Jones to deal with these queries but Constable Finney still had to supervise and it was really slowing him down. He needed to focus on the crime scenes of each burglary, writing up his findings and taking any witness statements.

"To be honest kids I don't think Constable Finney's got a clue who's done it, he just seems to be running around like a headless chicken" exclaimed Albert.

It was late afternoon and the children knew they still had to unpack and get ready for supper with Aunt May. This would mean dressing in their smart clothes and dining in the great hall. They both had their own bedrooms that were next to each other on the top floor. Apart from a couple of storage rooms, the top floor was their area. No one else used this floor so they could do as they pleased, within reason. All of their toys and brick-a-brac were kept up there in the playroom. Victoria was always telling them to tidy up their mess as it always looked as though a bomb had gone off in it. Aunt May's bedroom was on the first floor, it was the grandest of all the bedrooms with her adjoining walk in wardrobe and changing room, plus her en-suite bathroom. There were also four guest bedrooms on the first floor to accommodate any friends and family who may come to stay.

As the children passed through the kitchen on their way to their bedrooms, they saw Sylvia the cook preparing the evening meal.
"Hi Sylvia" shouted Thomas.

Sylvia gave a little shriek as she didn't hear the children come into the kitchen. "Oh you two, you gave me such a fright!" She put down the potato peeler and came over to give them a hug.

"Goodness look at you two, you're all grown up! And you're looking more and more like your parents!" she said.
"Mmm something smells good, what's on the menu tonight Sylvia?" asked Catherine
"Chicken soup, roast pork and vegetables and a lovely homemade sponge cake with cream for dessert" she replied.
Thomas and Catherine loved Sylvia's cooking and they knew she would spoil them with homemade cakes and deserts while they stayed at Ashbourne house.
The children said their goodbye's and carried on to their bedrooms.

At supper Thomas asked Aunt May if she was worried about all the burglaries and if Ashbourne House might be next!
"Oh no my dear Thomas I'm not worried and neither should you! I'm sure the police have everything under control, plus this old house is like a fortress, no one can get in if we don't want them to. Now I won't hear any more about it. I will get Charles to wake you early tomorrow as its market day and we need to be there early as it gets really busy".

The next morning Thomas and Catherine were already up and dressed as Charles came to wake them. They were excited about going to the market as they knew Aunt May was, she never missed it. She would normally get Charles to drive her there and meet up with her friends. But as Thomas and Catherine were staying with her, she would take them instead and she would drive the Bentley car into Pwllheli herself. After breakfast everyone was ready to go to the market, Charles escorted Aunt May and the children to the car and helped them in. Aunt May turned on the ignition and the Bentley roared into life. She released the handbrake and the Bentley shot off down the drive towards the main gate.

Nervously Catherine turned to Thomas "Hold on tight, it's going to be another white knuckle ride!" From previous outings with Aunt May in the Bentley, they knew that her driving wasn't the best and that she very rarely moved out of the way for other cars. She certainly didn't drive much, but always insisted when the children came to stay. After a few near misses and other drivers beeping and shaking their fists at them for nearly being forced off the road, they arrived at Pwllheli market in one piece.

The market was busy with the hustle and bustle of people buying and selling anything from local food to hardware goods, Persian rugs to children's handmade toys. Aunt May and the children slowly followed the procession of people down each narrow busy alley, market stall owners could be heard shouting out their latest bargains as they tried to entice potential customers to their stalls.

"Come and have a look at these quality towels ladies, if you buy one today, I'll throw in a matching flannel for free!" one man shouted as they passed by. They rounded the next corner and a gypsy woman with her head covered by a shawl, stopped Aunt May. "Come in dear, let me read your tarot cards for you" She said as she beckoned her towards a small tent. The door flap was tied back to reveal the dark area within. A small round table with a colourful table cloth stood in the middle of the tent with a chair either side. In the middle of the table was a crystal ball. Aunt May ignored the woman as she side stepped past her, dragging Catherine and Thomas along too! The gypsy woman shouted after them "How about I read the crystal ball and tell you your future?" When she got no reply from Aunt May, she went about trying her luck with the next unsuspecting passer-by.

After walking through most of the market, they all headed to a nearby cafe for tea and cakes. Aunt May had treated the children to some gifts. Thomas got a pair of binoculars and a new summer shirt. Catherine got a new diary, fountain pen with ink and a new summer dress.

Their rollercoaster ride back to Ashbourne House didn't take long; they turned into the sweeping driveway and made their way at break neck speed up to the house. Catherine spotted someone over near the woodshed; she tapped Thomas on the shoulder and pointed. Charles the butler was talking to two men; it looked like they were arguing as one was pointing at Charles. The two men looked shifty, one was tall, of medium build and the other was short and stocky. Catherine thought he resembled a beer barrel! The children couldn't see their faces as they had their backs to them. When they heard the Bentley approach, they pulled their trench coat collars up around their faces to hide themselves. This was strange as it was a warm summer's day, too warm for big heavy winter coats! The Bentley screeched to a halt outside the front doors. Everyone got out of the car, Thomas and Catherine looked over to the woodshed, they saw the two dark clothed men scurrying off into the fields and Charles briskly walking back to the house.

Thomas and Catherine ran inside to take their presents back to their bedrooms. They were on their way back outside to play in their favourite tree house that Albert had built them a few years before, when they spotted Charles in the hallway looking flustered. "Charles, who were those two men you were arguing with?" enquired Catherine. Charles looked surprised that he had been seen. "Two men, Oh err….. They were just some labourers who are working in the fields over summer". "What did they want? They looked angry with you" asked Thomas.
"Oh they were just angry they hadn't been paid yet" replied Charles laughing nervously. With that he turned to leave them, heading back towards the kitchen, then he stopped and looked back at the children.

"Don't you two worry about those men; it's all been sorted out now. So you don't need to concern your Aunt May about it" Then off he went.

"Why would he tell us not to mention it to Aunt May? I think we need to keep an eye on him Thomas, something smells fishy about all this". Thomas nodded in agreement as they both headed outside to the tree house to play.

Chapter 4

That evening the two children sat in Catherine's bedroom, they were already in their pyjamas' and dressing gowns, ready for bed. They talked about the day's events. Thomas laughed rubbing his neck, "Let's hope we don't have to drive with Aunt May anytime soon. My neck is hurting; it feels like I've been driving a Grand Prix racing car!"

They discussed the two shady men who were arguing with Charles. They had to whisper as they knew Charles would be knocking on the door any minute, delivering coco and biscuits. They didn't want him to hear them discussing the two men. Then sure enough there was a 'Tap Tap' at the door and in walked Charles, carrying a silver tray with two mugs of coco and a plate of homemade biscuits on it. He sat the tray down on the bedside table. "Will there be anything else children?" he asked. "Err no thank you Charles, that's just fine" replied Catherine.
"Very well Miss Catherine, once you've had your

coco make sure you brush your teeth before bed please". The children both agreed so Charles left, closing the bedroom door behind him. The children remained quiet until they could hear him retreating down the corridor to the stairs, they then continued with their conversation about the two men from this afternoon. "Charles looked scared today when he was arguing with those two men didn't he?" said Catherine.

"Yeah and did you notice the bigger of the two men was doing all the shouting and pointing, he must be in charge eh?" added Thomas.

"Did you see Charles' face when he realised we'd seen him, he almost turned as white as a sheet. He certainly didn't want Aunt May to find out, which makes me think he's keeping something from us" said Catherine. Thomas agreed "Yeah he's definitely up to something!"

They both ate their biscuits and drank their coco, then Thomas headed off to his own bedroom as Catherine wanted to write down everything that had happened into her new diary.

The following day the children were up early as usual, they washed and dressed in the clothes Victoria had laid out for them both the night before, then headed downstairs. As it was early, the dining hall wasn't ready for breakfast yet, so the children ate in the kitchen. Fortunately Sylvia the cook always seemed to be up before them, preparing food for the day ahead. She made them porridge, toast with jam and glasses of fresh orange juice. She asked them if they had enjoyed the market yesterday. The children told her it had been good but busy with holiday makers as is usual at this time of year. They showed her what Aunt May had bought them as well.

After breakfast Thomas and Catherine headed outside into the warm sunshine. There was a haze of mist hanging over the garden and surrounding fields but the sun was slowly burning the last of the evening dampness away. They decided to go and play on the main beach which was a few minutes away. They walked down the sweeping driveway, past the large stone pillars at the entrance and across the lane onto the golden sand dunes. They brought their bucket and spade's so they could build a sand castle village. Also they had a crab line so they could try and catch some crabs later in the afternoon. Thomas always had to take charge when building the sand castle village, the castle had to have a moat and a draw bridge made from sticks and the village buildings had to be within the castle walls, "in case of attack" Thomas would say. He took the building of the village very seriously and got annoyed when Catherine teased him saying "Who's going to attack us, the seagulls or the crab we catch?"

Building the village took up most of the morning, they got it finished before the tide came back in. "I'm getting bored with this now Thomas. Let's try and catch some crabs" With a sigh Thomas reluctantly agreed, but not before he stood back and marvelled at their sandcastle village. "What a masterpiece" he exclaimed. They then left the village to the mercy of the inevitable high tide and marched over to the rocks.

Catherine had kept some toast from breakfast, she unfolded her handkerchief to show Thomas "this can be our bait".

"That's great, put some water on it and make it into a ball then it will stay on the hook better" ordered Thomas. The children climbed onto the slippery rocks and slowly made their way to the sea edge. Catherine hooked on the bread balls and cast the line into the sea. Meanwhile Thomas took one of the buckets and filled it with sea water from a nearby rock pool, ready to put any crabs they caught into it. Ten minutes went by and the children had had no luck. Thomas was tutting to himself as he got a wet foot after slipping into the sea, the crab line had got caught on a clump of seaweed and Catherine had made him go and retrieve it. So they decided to climb carefully over the rocks and move further down the coast to a new spot. A further 20 minutes went by and still no crabs, by now the children were getting bored.

"Looks like all the crabs are still in bed eh?" said Thomas. So they wound up the crab line and moved on, until they reached a cove with a small stretch of beach instead of rocks. Further up the beach the tall cliffs had been split open by thousands of years of pounding sea's, to reveal a big dark cave.

"That's cool, let's go and investigate" said Thomas.

"But we won't be able to see anything in there it's so dark! Tell you what, let's go in as far as we can until it's too dark then we turn back. Anyway it might not be that big" said Catherine.

"Ok let's go before the tide comes in too far" agreed Thomas.

The children walked into the mouth of the cave slowly and carefully to make sure they didn't trip over any rocks. They could feel the temperature drop as they moved out of the sun and into the damp shade of the cave. They hadn't gone far when Thomas said "Blimey I can't see a thing!"

"Feel for the cave wall and wait for your eyes to adjust to the dark, it won't take long" said Catherine. Soon the children's eyes started to adjust to the dark, so with the help of the wall they edged further into the cave.

"Err the walls are all wet and slimey" said Catherine.

"I think I feel seaweed, well I hope its seaweed!" replied Thomas. The children were about 20 metres into the cave when suddenly Thomas, who was leading gave out a yelp as he fell over something.

"Ouch! I've stubbed my toe on something".

"Are you alright? What was it, a rock?" asked Catherine.

"No it feels like a wooden box, a crate maybe, hold on I can feel another one, no make that two! I can feel some metal objects next to the crates, I'll try and find something small enough to put in my pocket and bring out to the daylight, it's probably just some old rusty metal!" he said.

Chapter 5

Thomas told Catherine to start edging her way along the wall back towards the entrance. They stumbled out of the cave into the sunlight. "Ahh my eyes, the sunshine is hurting my eyes!" exclaimed Thomas.

"Mine too!" replied Catherine.

As they were waiting for their eyes to adjust back to normal, which seemed to be taking forever, they heard someone shout "Oi, you two!" They looked towards the direction of the yell, their blurry vision could just about make out two figures in the distance running towards them.

"How are your eyes, can you see properly?" asked Catherine eagerly.

"Yeah pretty much!" replied Thomas rubbing them.

"Well let's get moving then, I don't think those men are stopping us to ask for the time and I don't want to hang about to see what they want!

They must have something to do with those crates in the cave and they have just seen us come out of there, quick make for the cliffs!" shouted Catherine.

Thomas didn't need to be asked twice, he left his bucket and spade at the mouth of the cave and was off like a shot, with Catherine following closely behind.

By now the two men were clambering over the first set of rocks and making their way to the section of beach in front of the cave entrance. Further along the headland Thomas and Catherine had made it successfully over some very slippery rocks and to the foot of the cliff face. They knew this cliff face pretty well as they had scaled it a few times before. There were two or three routes that could be negotiated to safely get around the cliffs to the beach on the other side. Thomas and Catherine had already headed for the route they knew was the easiest and quickest. But they knew it was still quite hazardous, they would be climbing quite high.

They didn't actually know but Thomas estimated it was the height of a house. One slip or wrong step could leave them with a serious fall onto the rocks below resulting in broken limbs or worse! Plus they had the added pressure of being pursued by two unknown men.

With Catherine leading they climbed up about five feet and made it to the first of a series of ledges that spanned across the cliff face. This first ledge was no wider than the length of the children's feet, so they had to keep close to the cliff face. Thomas and Catherine made steady progress and were at the end of the ledge, when they could hear the two men arrive at the foot of the cliff. They could hear the men arguing about who would go first. One man shouted "Just get going will you, if two kids can do it, it'll be easy for us!"

The other man replied "Yeah but have you seen them climb, they're like bloody monkeys!"

Thomas and Catherine had now climbed up onto the second ledge. Both breathing heavily after the demanding climb so far, they decide to stop and catch their breath and survey how the two men were doing. As they peered down below them it was clear the men weren't as agile as Thomas and Catherine. They were finding the climbing tough going and they didn't know the route to take. Catherine tapped Thomas on the shoulder, "O.k. you know the hard bit is next then we're home free!"

"Let's get it done and get off this damn cliff!" replied Thomas.

The 'Hard bit' referred to a missing part of the ledge further up ahead. Approximately two feet of rock was missing, so a running jump to the other side was required. Down on the ground the children knew a jump that wide would be easy, but up on the side of the cliff it was a different, more dangerous scenario altogether. They didn't have the usual amount of time to psyche themselves up and wait for the wind to die down. They would have to jump and pray all went well.

Catherine went first; she edged to the end of the ledge to take one quick look, and then took two steps back. She ran and jumped and in a blink of an eye her feet made contact with the rock ledge on the other side. She immediately clung onto any part of the rock face she could to stop her momentum taking her too far. She gave a big sigh of relief, shuffled a few paces further then turned back towards her brother and beckoned him over with a wave of her hand. Thomas made the same brief checks as Catherine had, then ran and jumped. As he landed on the opposite ledge his shoulder scraped the cliff face knocking him off balance slightly. He began to fall off the ledge and panicked, trying to grab hold of anything he could.

"Ahh Catherine, Help!" he screamed.

Without time to think, Catherine grabbed hold of his shirt with one hand and with all her might pulled him back, slamming Thomas into the rock face with a thud!

"Phew! Thanks sis, I thought I was a goner then!"

"It's alright, now let's get going!" she replied.

Thomas' frightening episode had let the two men catch up and they were slowly edging their way along the first ledge. They helped each other up onto the second ledge, just as Thomas and Catherine disappeared around the corner of the cliff and out of sight. The two men got to the gap in the second ledge, the first man easily jumped across but the second shorter fatter man hesitated. As he jumped he stumbled and fell across the gap, his chest thumped into the edge of the ledge hard. In his pain and panic he shrieked out loud and scrambled to stop himself from falling. "John, help me or I'm gonna fall!" he screamed. "Ahh, Sid stop messing around the kids are getting away!" replied the other man.

He grabbed his mate by the arm and heaved him back up onto the ledge. "Now come on or we'll lose them!" hissed the man known as John.

So the two men shuffled along to the end of the ledge and climbed around the corner of the cliff face.

By now Thomas and Catherine had made it to some steps that lead down to a beach. The steps had been carved out of the rock by the owners of a house up on the cliff top above.

The children raced down the steps and ran across the beach heading towards the harbour. As they ran, Catherine glanced back to see the two men climbing around the corner of the cliff.

"They're still hot on our tails; they're not giving up easily! We'll have to hide somewhere in the harbour" she shouted to Thomas. He nodded in agreement, "Let's hurry!"

They raced to some steps which ran up the side of the harbour wall to the top. On the other side lay the harbour itself. It was in the shape of a horse shoe, with a walkway running all around it. Protruding from the centre of the harbours walkway were two wooden jetties. Boats of all shapes and sizes were tied up to the jetties in designated, numbered bays. There were rowing boats, pleasure boats of the rich, fishing boats and even the coast guard boat.

The busy harbour was also home to a large flock of seagulls. They could be heard squawking at each other as they jostled for space on posts and railings. They were waiting for the next fishing boat to enter the harbour with its daily catch, hoping to get fish scraps off the boats deck or anything that might be thrown over the side.

As Thomas and Catherine ran onto the walkway they scanned the harbour for somewhere to hide, then headed over to one of the wooden jetties. "Duck!" shouted Thomas. So they both dropped down behind a stack of crab pots. As they slowly peered up from behind them, they could see the two men coming down the harbour wall steps. They ducked back down again and looked around for a better hiding place. Then Thomas spotted it,

"Look over there, that's where we can hide!" he whispered.

Catherine followed his pointing finger towards a small fishing boat with a dirty green sheet covering the boats deck. Catherine nodded then whispered back "Come on let's go!"

One by one they crawled on hands and knees over to the boat. Thomas lifted a flap of the sheet up so Catherine could climb in, then he got in himself and pulled the flap of the sheet back over the top of them. It was dark and extremely hot under the sheet and the smell was overpowering! "Urrh it stinks of fish under here, I think I'm gonna be sick!" exclaimed Thomas holding his nose.

"Shh Thomas, they could be close and hear you. Be quiet and keep still" ordered his sister.

The children lay on their sides, propped up on one elbow in the quiet darkness listening out for the men. Time seemed to stop as they waited, trying to keep still. They both started to sweat in the smelly humid conditions beneath the sheet.

Then they heard it, quiet at first but then slowly getting louder, the sound of footsteps on the wooden jetty. In fear Catherine grabbed Thomas' free hand with hers. The footsteps were loud and clear now; they were right next to the boat. They could hear the wooden boards of the jetty creaking as someone moved about. Then the sheet started to rustle and move. Suddenly there was brilliant bright daylight. The cover had been thrust back off the boats deck, revealing Thomas and Catherine cowering in the corner. They tensed their little bodies, waiting for the worst.

"Hey, what are you two doing in there?" shouted a shocked voice.

The puzzled children looked up to see two fishermen staring down at them.

"Sorry sir, two men were chasing us and we were scared, so we hid in your boat!" explained Catherine.

"That's alright young lady, for a minute there me and Charlie thought we had stowaways!" laughed one of the fishermen.

"Here let's help you out of there" added the second fishermen.

The children were reluctant to get out of the boat. Sensing this, the first fisherman said "Oh don't worry, we saw those men leaving the harbour in the direction of the village."

"Was one tall and the other short and fat?" asked the second fisherman.

"Yeah that's them!" replied Thomas

Relieved they had gone; Thomas and Catherine stood up and were helped off the boat back onto the jetty. They apologised once more to the fishermen then headed for the harbour entrance, leaving the men to load their boat up with equipment for their fishing trip.

The children ran down the jetty and stopped at the harbour entrance. They peered around the corner and could just make out the two men in the distance, walking quickly towards the village.

"Phew! Thank goodness, looks like they are finally off our trail" said Catherine.
"Well let's not hang around just in case they change their minds. Let's head for the bus stop and get back to Ashbourne house!" replied Thomas.

So they ran down the road in the opposite direction to the men, crossed over and went and sat down at the bus stop bench to wait patiently for the next bus.

Ten minutes later the No.11 bus to Pwllheli came trundling along the road.
"Ah finally it's here Catherine!" said Thomas holding out his arm so the bus would stop. The children climbed on-board and the conductor took their money for the fare and gave them each a ticket. The children went and slumped on the nearest seat as the bus set off.

"Did you get a good look at those men?" Thomas asked his sister.

"No I was too busy trying to get away from them, why did you?"

"No not really but they looked very similar to the two men who were arguing with Charles" he replied.

"Well they must have something to do with those crates, they were chasing after us the moment they saw us come out of the cave. They must have been coming to check they hadn't been discovered" said Catherine.

"I'm just relieved they didn't catch us, who knows what they might have done!"

"It doesn't bare thinking about" said Catherine as they both sat back in their seats and waited for their stop to arrive. Suddenly Thomas jolted forward remembering something.

"Hold on a minute, I forgot about this!"

He rummaged in his shorts pocket and pulled out a handful of sand and the metal object he'd

found in the cave.
"Blimey, look at this!" he said.

In his hand lay a gold broach which was encrusted with rubies and diamonds. The red and white of the precious stones and the polished gold sparkled and shone, lighting up the inside of the bus. Thomas quickly cupped his hands together, covering the broach. The children both sheepishly looked around the bus to see the other passengers looking back at them curiously. So they both just smiled and faced back towards the front of the bus.

"Better put that back in your pocket until we get home, we don't want anyone getting suspicious!" said Catherine, secretly pointing in the direction of the other passengers. So Thomas put it back in his pocket.
"Let's delay telling anyone about the events of today until we can get a good look inside those crates, agreed?" said Catherine
Thomas nodded.

Once off the bus and walking back up the driveway to Ashbourne house, they decided that it would be too late to go back to the cave with torches as it would now be the afternoon high tide. The sea would be lapping at the cave entrance if not already inside and it would just be too dangerous to try and get in there. So they would have to go first thing in the morning at low tide.

Chapter 6

When the next morning eventually arrived, the children made sure they were at the cave at low tide so they had plenty of time to search it. They had borrowed torches from the kitchen utility room. Each had a satchel just in case they found more items that they could pass onto the police. Now with the help of the torches, the children had no problem seeing in the dark cave. As they shone them around, they could see the green slimey wet walls that had helped them to navigate in and out of the cave yesterday. The walls rose steeply upwards to the roof of the cave. There were strands of seaweed and bits of old fishermen's netting that had caught on sharp parts of the wall when the high tide had swept them into the cave, and they were now left hanging from the walls like decorations. Once they were where they thought the gold broach and three crates had been found, they shone their torches around. "I don't understand Catherine; it's all gone, but where?"
"The burglars must have moved them

somewhere else. I bet they were scared we might have told the police what we had found. Look here! There are more foot prints in the sand. Let's follow them back out of the cave, see where they go" said Catherine. The children followed the foot prints back out to near the cave entrance, and then they stopped.
"The tide has washed the rest of them away. I can't believe they managed to move the crates at high tide, they must have had help!" said Thomas. Catherine shrugged her shoulders "Well they're long gone now and there is nothing more for us to do here. Come on let's go back to the house".

The children trudged back to Ashbourne house feeling deflated. They expected the crates to be still there for them to have broken open, revealing the stolen 'loot' from all the burglaries. Then they could have told the police of their find and be the heroes of the village. But instead they were back to square one, only having the gold broach as any real evidence of what might have been in the cave.

Chapter 7

They tried to cheer themselves up by playing cowboy and Indians in the garden. Thomas was the cowboy and he was up in the tree house, pretending it was a fort. Catherine was the Indian and she was down in the garden, she had made a Wigwam out of sticks and an old bed sheet Victoria the house keeper had given them. It was Catherine's job to attack the fort seeing as she was the Indian. Thomas was keeping look out for her using the binoculars that Aunt May had bought him at Pwllheli market a few days before.

Catherine was skipping around the bottom of the tree house on her horse; this was a broom with the shape of a horse's head made out of cardboard, taped to the broom. She was shouting at the top of her voice while patting her mouth, like Indians did in the movies. Plus she had her trusty bow and arrows and was wearing an old scarf around her head with feathers stuck in it. She had red and white painted patterns on her face with paint found in the playroom. An old towel with a hole cut in it for her head, made a good Indian dress which was finished off with a belt. Thomas was wearing his cowboy hat, a checked shirt, neckerchief and waistcoat and a pair of shorts. He was firing his cap guns down at Catherine, trying to fend her off. Eventually Catherine retreated to the safety of her Wigwam so she could plan her next attack.

Thomas was keeping an eye on his enemy through his binoculars, when something caught his eye! He moved his binoculars from his sisters Wigwam over to the fields behind her. As the breeze made the wheat sway back and forth in the wheat field, he could see something glinting amongst it. At first he thought it was nothing, but the more he concentrated on it the more the sunshine made it sparkle. He shouted down to his sister "Catherine come up here and take a look at this!" Catherine ran over from her Wigwam and climbed up the ladders of the tree house to Thomas.

"What is it?"

"Look through my binoculars into that field over there, can you see something sparkling?" he asked.

Catherine took the binoculars and aimed them in the direction of the field, after a few moments of searching she spotted something glinting.

"Yes I can see it; it's just some old metal isn't it?"

"No it's reflecting too brightly, to me it looks like silver or something! Come on let's go and investigate" Thomas replied.

The children climbed down from the tree house and headed back to the house to get changed and cleaned up. They then made their way over to the wheat field. It took them a good fifteen minutes to get to the area where they saw the shiny object. They had to search around for a while because the wheat was waist high, and it was difficult to see their feet on the ground. They decided to split up so they could search a larger area. It wasn't long before Catherine shouted out

"Thomas, over here. I think I've found it!" Thomas waded through the wheat towards Catherine. As he got to Catherine she almost disappeared into the wheat, as she bent down to pick up the object. When she stood up, she held a large silver candle stick holder in her hands.
"I nearly tripped over it" she said.
"See I told you it wasn't just some old metal. But what's a candle stick holder doing all the way out here?" Said Thomas puzzled.
"Well it doesn't take a genius to work that one out. My guess is it's been dropped by the burglars. I bet they've passed through this field with those crates last night, searching for a new hiding place" replied Catherine.
"Come on let's take it back to the house I think it's time we spoke to Albert, he'll know what to do, plus he might know if there are any derelict buildings nearby where they could hide out" said Thomas.

Back at Albert's shed; the children showed him the candle stick holder they had just found plus the broach from the cave. They also explained how they had found the large crates in the cave, and then were chased by two men into the harbour but managed to escape. Then when they went back this morning to the cave the crates had gone.

"Blimey, who were these men? Did you recognise them?"

The children both shock their heads. Albert stood their rubbing his chin, deep in thought then turned to Thomas and Catherine.

"Well you need to go and tell your aunt what you told me and show her the things you've found. She needs to know what's going on! Then she will probably send you to tell the police as well, the sooner they know the better chance they have of trying to apprehend them!"

So they all headed inside to find Aunt May. In the kitchen Sylvia was busy preparing lunch for Aunt May and some of her friends.

"Sylvia do you know where our aunt is?" asked Catherine.

"I'm afraid I don't Miss Catherine, I'd ask Charles. He greeted your aunt's friends on their arrival not more than half an hour ago" replied the cook.

So Albert and the children headed off in to the hallway to find Charles. They eventually found him coming out of the drawing room.
"Hello Charles can you tell me where our aunt is please" asked Thomas.
"Yes your aunt and her friends are in the dining room awaiting lunch" replied the butler, then he spotted Albert as well.
"Why are you here Albert, haven't you got work to be doing?"
"Yes I have Charles, but Thomas and Catherine asked me to accompany them to see their aunt which is what I am doing!" exclaimed Albert, a little annoyed.

Charles just stood there with his hands clasped behind his back
"Your aunt doesn't want to be disturbed until after lunch".
"Well this can't wait!" shouted Catherine as she

turned and ran off down the hall towards the dining room.

Thomas and Albert looked at one another then both turned and ran after Catherine. Charles wasn't expecting them all to run, so he was slow to react and follow.

Catherine arrived at the dining room; she knocked on the big oak door and waited for her aunt to answer. Once she did Catherine opened the door and entered just as Thomas and Albert had caught her up. Thomas bounded straight into the dining room after his sister, while Albert waited patiently outside in the hall. Out of breath the children tried to explain to their aunt what was going on and what they had found. But they were both panting and talking over one another and obviously not making any sense.
"Children slow down and catch your breath!" said Aunt May. By now Charles had appeared at the dining room doorway, out of breath himself and a little red faced! "I apologies for the interruption

Lady Ripley, I did tell the children you were not to be disturbed" he said.

"It's alright Charles I'll take it from here, right you two lets go over to the study so you can tell me what this is all about. Excuse me ladies while I talk to my niece and nephew. If lunch arrives please start without me, I won't be long" she said.

They all walked across the hallway and into the study. The children by then had caught their breath and explained everything that had happened and had shown her the items they had found in the cave and field respectively.

"They came to me ma'am wondering what to do, so I suggested they come and tell you straight away. I took one look at that candle stick holder and knew it was worth a bob or two! It was obvious it hadn't been dropped there by accident!" said Albert. Their aunt was shocked and demanded to drive the children to the police station herself!

"No! Err ....it's alright Aunt May you have guests here" intervened Thomas quickly. Relieved by her brothers quick thinking, Catherine added "Yes it's alright; we can ride into the village ourselves".

Aunt May reluctantly agreed with them, she then studied the items closely.
"I find it worrying that this was found in our fields" she said holding up the silver candle stick. "What else or who else is hiding out on our land?"

"Right get these items to the police station; tell them everything you've told me. When you're done come straight back home, no dilly dallying do you understand children?"
"Yes Aunt May, we will leave straight away" replied Thomas.

So everyone left the study, Aunt May went back to her guests, Albert went back to his work and the children went up to their rooms to find a satchel to carry the candlestick and broach in.
"Thank goodness we talked Aunt May out of driving us to the police station, we've had enough

excitement for one day!" exclaimed Catherine. Chuckling Thomas agreed and pretended to wipe sweat from his brow.

Once at their bedrooms, Thomas turned to his sister and demanded "I'm the boy therefore I'll carry the satchel!"

Catherine laughed "Well I'm the oldest so I should carry it! I tell you what we'll flip a coin for it. Heads you take it, Tails I take it, deal?" Thomas nodded in agreement.

So Catherine flipped the coin high into the air then caught it in one hand and slapped it onto the back of the other hand keeping it covered.
"Ready?" she asked
"Yes!" he replied.

She slowly raised her hand to reveal the coin resting on the back of the other one.
"Ah hah, tails, I win I take the satchel" said Catherine triumphantly.
"Damn!" Thomas replied grumpily.

Once that had been sorted out, the children raced out of the house and over to the shed that housed their bikes.

Chapter 8

Abersoch was busy with the hustle and bustle of a seaside village. The locals were getting on with their daily business, while the holiday makers were making the most of the fine weather and mulling about doing the holiday thing. Like dining in the restaurants and cafes, buying souvenirs and beach equipment like bats and balls or buckets and spades. Thomas and Catherine rode into Abersoch and up to the police station. They lent their bikes up against the front of the station and went inside. Constable Jones, fresh out of police school was manning the counter.

"Excuse me Constable, our aunt, Lady Ripley at Ashbourne House has asked us to come in and show you what we have found near the house. It may have something to do with all those burglaries that have happened" said Catherine.

"Alright children, what is it you have to show me?" replied Constable Jones.

"Go on Catherine, show him what we have found!" ordered Thomas.

So Catherine took the satchel off her shoulder and opened it. First she pulled out the silver candlestick and placed it on the counter, then she pulled out the gold jewel encrusted broach and placed it beside the candlestick. While she did this, Thomas mentioned the chase that had happened earlier with the two men. Once he'd finished and the two items sat in front of them on the counter, the children stood back and looked at Constable Jones, eagerly awaiting his response.

The constable looked at the items in front of him for a moment, "Gosh! These look extremely expensive. Where exactly did you find them again?"

The children told the constable everything they had told their aunt and Albert earlier. They had to keep stopping as the constable was writing a statement and was struggling to keep up. Every so often he would have to stop and massage his aching writing hand. Then he would start taking notes again only responding with "Uh Hmm" or a brief question to gain more information. Once they had given their account to the constable, he put down his pencil, which was nearly blunt after completing the mammoth statement. He read it back to the children, checking nothing had been missed. When they agreed it was all there, Constable Jones let out a loud sigh "Phew! Right I'll need to take the items as evidence. I will let Constable Finney see them and read the statement on his return to the station. He will be very interested to know about the two men who chased you in to the harbour. If he requires anymore information I'm sure he will come and see you. Now if you will excuse me children, I need to go and type up your statement". With that the children said goodbye and left the station.

Back outside in the sunshine, Thomas and Catherine wondered what to do with themselves. "I know Aunt May said to go straight back when

we'd spoken to the police, but I think we should do some investigating ourselves. You know ask around and what not!" said Thomas.
"Yes alright, we could go to the Newsagents first, ask some questions and buy ourselves some sweets while we're there!"
"Great idea sis!" he replied.

So they retrieved their bikes and pushed them along to the Newsagents further down the high street. They asked the man behind the counter if he had heard anything or seen anyone suspicious, while they picked their sweets.

"I'm afraid I haven't heard anything. I only know what has been printed in the local paper! And there are so many strangers knocking about at this time of year, you know holiday makers! They all look suspicious with their red sunburnt faces, looking like lobsters!" sniggered the man.

The children realised that the newsagent knew less than they did, so they paid for their sweets and left. They decided to move on to Mr Williams the Butcher before they set off for home, plus it was only next door!

Mr Williams was serving a customer as the children entered the shop, so they patiently waited their turn. Once he had handed over the customers meat, took her money and bided her good afternoon he turned to the children.
"Good afternoon children, you look familiar, that's it! Your Lady Ripley's niece and nephew aren't you! I remember you being with her at the summer fate last year, although you've grown up since then! Surely your aunt hasn't eaten all that meat Charles bought last weekend!" said the butcher.

Thomas and Catherine explained that they weren't there to buy meat.
"You've obviously heard about all those burglaries that have happened. Have you heard any gossip or seen anyone suspicious?" enquired Thomas.
"Well yes I have heard a few things as it happens" he said. Then he told them what he had

Told Constable Finney the day before.

"John Evans up at Peak Farm was telling me that someone or something has been at his chicken coop. A load of eggs and three chickens have gone missing and he suspects a fox. But he can't see where it's been getting into the coop plus there is no sign of a struggle, you know feathers and blood! So he's keeping a closer eye out, just in case it's not a fox and someone is breaking in and stealing them. Then there's Peter Edwards the baker, someone tried to steal his delivery van a few nights ago. Only something scared them off, they made a right mess of the driver's door trying to get in. He's really annoyed as he hasn't had it long!"

"Really, that is interesting; no one has actually seen the men responsible for the burglaries. My guess is it's them who have stolen the chickens and tried to steal the van!" declared Thomas.

"Hold on young man, no one can be certain of that, so let's not jump to conclusions just yet. Let Constable Finney get on with his enquiries first" replied Mr Williams.

"Alright Mr Williams thanks for the information, we best be getting back home, our aunt will be wondering where we are!" said Catherine.

So they headed for the door. Then Catherine stopped and turned back to the butcher and asked "Excuse me Mr Williams, where exactly is Peak Farm?"
"Why it's not far from Ashbourne House if my memory serves me right, your land and his are adjoining!" he replied.

Chapter 9

When the children got back to Ashbourne House they went to find Albert as they had a few questions for him. They found him cutting the lawn with his petrol engine mower. They told him what Mr Williams the butcher had told them.

"Is there any unused buildings on the Ashbourne estate that the burglars could be hiding in?" asked Catherine.
"You're the third person to ask me that question!" replied Albert
"Really, who else has asked you?" said Thomas inquisitively.
"First Constable Finney came round this morning asking about the land, so I showed him the map I have in my shed. It shows all of the Ashbourne estate with all buildings and out houses. So he got permission from your aunt to go and have a look around" said Albert.
"Who was the second person then Albert?" Catherine enquired.

Albert took a handkerchief from his pocket and rubbed sweat from the back of his neck.
"Well there's the strange thing, it was Charles! When I asked why he wanted to see the map, he said there was some work that needed to be carried out and he needed to see where exactly on the land it was. When I said that I hadn't heard of any work taking place, he got all defensive and said your aunt had asked him to sort it out. I don't know what old Charlie boy is up to!" Thomas looked at Catherine "Yes what is he up to I wonder?"

The children followed Albert to his shed to have a look at the map. He got it out of a draw and unrolled it on his work bench, putting empty cups on each corner to stop it curling up. Then they all peered over it. It was an old looking map, a bit tatty around the edges. In the top left hand corner it read 'Land Registry' for Ashbourne House date: 1902.
"Why have you got this map in your shed Albert, isn't it an important document?" asked Catherine.
"There was a dispute a couple of years ago with a

neighbouring farmer over boundaries, so I needed the map to establish where the edge of the land was so I could put up some fencing. Anyway this map is only a copy; I think the original is in your Aunt's safe" replied Albert.
"Constable Finney took an interest in this one here" he said pointing at a building.
"It's the old hunting lodge; it's close to a little dirt track that runs in between your aunt's land and Peak Farm. He said he was going to drive up there and have a look around!" explained Albert.

"What about this one here?" asked Thomas
"Ah that's an old barn, but it's not that close to the dirt track! Constable Finney didn't seem bothered about it" replied Albert.
"Maybe we should go and have a look at it, just in case they are using it as a hideout or for storage. You never know!" said Catherine.
"Yeah, good idea sis, But I need to eat first. There's no way I could go all that way on an empty stomach!" exclaimed Thomas.

As they left Albert's shed for the main house, Albert shouted them back. "Hey you two, you've forgotten the map! You won't get far without it! I've just checked the map again and realised that the last four burglaries all circled Ashbourne House. My guess is they may have moved the crates last night because you two showed up at the cave. Maybe they are getting all their 'loot' together in one hiding place, then preparing to get out of Abersoch while they can. This could be very dangerous children; we don't know how ruthless these men could be if they think they've been found. I think it would be best to wait for me to finish my duties then I'll come with you!" said Albert.

The children told him that it would be too late by then. But they promised him that if they saw or heard anything they would turn around and come straight back and find him.

Chapter 10

After their sandwiches supplied by Sylvia, Thomas and Catherine headed for the old derelict barn. They took a satchel with a drink, Thomas's binoculars and Albert's old map. Albert estimated it would take them about half an hour or so to get there, providing they followed the map.

The children had been walking for about fifteen minutes and the hot afternoon sun was starting to tire them out, so they decided to stop for a rest under the shade of a nearby tree. Thomas took out the map and a bottle of Sylvia's homemade lemon squash.
"Judging by the map I think we have about twenty minutes left to walk, and then we should be there" said Catherine.
"Looks like there should be a stream up ahead that we'll have to cross, hope it's not too deep" replied Thomas as he looked over Catherine's shoulder at the map.

It wasn't long before they arrived at the stream. It was about five metres wide and too big to jump across without getting wet! Luckily the stream wasn't deep and weeks of hot summer weather had shrunk the stream to a trickle. So Catherine and Thomas could walk across the dry river bed and hop over the stream. They climbed up the river bank on the other side and dusted themselves down. They could see the old derelict barn through the trees in the distance, so they set off for it. The barn had definitely seen better days. It looked like it had been un-used for many years. Part of the roof had fallen in after a nearby tree's branch must have snapped off and hit it in an old storm some years before. There was moss and ivy covering what remained of the roof. Ivy and shrubs covered or hid most of the barn walls, but the barn door was just visible.

Thomas crouched down behind a nearby bush and pulled Catherine down with him.
"Ouch! What are you doing?" she shouted at him.
"Shh, remember what Albert said. Don't get too close to the barn just in case the burglars are in

there. Let's just hide here for a moment, I'll have a look at the barn through my binoculars and check the coast is clear so we can go and have a look inside." Catherine nodded in agreement. So Thomas rummaged inside the satchel and pulled out his binoculars. He put them to his eyes and focused in on the barn in the distance. Once he was happy it looked empty, they slowly crept over to the barn door being careful where they stood. They didn't want to stand on any twigs that would snap and reveal they were there!

It took both of them to force open the big door, the rusty door hinges creaked loudly as the door moved. They could only get it open a jar as it probably hadn't been touched in some time, but it was enough for the children to squeeze through into the barn.

Inside the barn it was dark even with some of the roof missing. A smell of rotting wood and dampness hung in the air. Birds had built nests in what was left of the roof and spider's webs hung all over the place.

"Err yuck!" screamed Catherine, wiping the remains of a spiders web from her face and hair. "Ha, nice look you've got there sis!" Thomas giggled.

The floor of the barn was covered in bushes and small sapling trees; it was like a miniature forest. There was a clearing at one corner of the barns floor and what looked like the remains of a camp fire lay there. There were lots of stones made into a circular shape with burnt wood in the middle. Next to the old camp fire remains lay a bundle of sticks that would have been used to keep the fire going. A couple of old log stumps also lay around the fire; these would have been makeshift stools for someone to sit on. The children couldn't tell when the camp fire was last used but it didn't look that long ago.

"I wonder if it was some poachers using this barn while hunting for rabbits or birds. There are bones and feathers here but I don't know what bird they belong to, maybe a chicken but who knows!" said Catherine as she examined the remains.

"It could have been those burglars, but it looks like they've abandoned it now and moved on, I don't think they'll use this place again. Come on let's get out of here and head back home, this place is giving me the creeps!" replied Thomas.

The children squeezed back past the big barn door, then both put all their effort into getting the door shut again. As they headed off from the barn, Catherine turned to Thomas "Well that just leaves the old hunting lodge. Maybe we could go and check it tomorrow?"
Thomas agreed "come on let's get going, it's a long walk back to Ashbourne House."

Un-be known to the children they were being watched from a nearby bush.
"I told you those kids would come snooping around. If you hadn't been so rubbish at climbing that cliff face yesterday Sid, we would have caught em!" whispered the taller man
"Well it's a good job we moved from that barn and found the old lodge eh John!" said the short barrelled man.

"Yeah for once Sid your right" replied the taller man.

"Come on John, now they're onto us; let's just stick to the plan and leave tomorrow night. Get the boat to pick us and the 'loot' up off Abersoch beach as arranged and we'll be scot free, drinking beers on a sunny beach somewhere!" Said Sid

"I've told you Sid, there's one more job we're gonna do before we get out of here and that's Ashbourne House, and I'm not leaving until we've done it. There's some valuable stuff in there and I want it!" replied John. With that they crept away from the derelict barn and headed back to the old hunting lodge to plan the burglary of Ashbourne House.

Chapter 11

By the time Thomas and Catherine arrived back home it was tea time, so they headed straight inside to wash their hands. As they rushed into the dining room, Aunt May was already waiting.
"Ah hello you two, what have you been up to today, anything exciting?"
"Oh yes thank you Aunt May, we've had a great day. We're a little tired now so it will be early to bed tonight!" replied Catherine
"Make sure you have baths before you go to bed, we can't have grubby children at bedtime can we!"
"We will Aunt May" replied both children.

Charles entered the room pushing a trolley of food made by Sylvia the cook. He set about serving the food onto plates and placing them down in front of Aunt May and the children. As he was doing so, Catherine chirped up "Albert was showing Thomas and me the map of Ashbourne House today Aunt May!"

Charles nearly dropped the plate he was holding. He gave Catherine a look of shock before composing himself and carrying on serving the food.

"Why did he show you that old thing children?" enquired Aunt May

"Oh no real reason, he was just showing us how much land you have and where all the buildings are" replied Catherine.

As his sister spoke, Thomas watched Charles closely. It was obvious he was paying a lot of attention to the ongoing conversation, more than serving the evening meal!

Once they were finished and excused from the table, Thomas and Catherine made their way up to their rooms to get ready for bed. They met a flustered looking Charles who stopped them at the foot of the stairs.

"Just before you retire for the evening, I would just like to say that it isn't a good idea to venture too far from the house in search of adventure. Especially near those derelict buildings, they are old and could be unstable. It would be very dangerous children".

"It's alright Charles, we have been over there today looking around the old barn!" replied Thomas.

"Oh, have you... Did you find anything interesting?"

"No we didn't, like you said Charles, they're just derelict!" intervened Catherine.

"Well as I said it's a good idea to stay away from those old buildings" said Charles and he was off down the hallway before either of them could reply.

"What was that all about?" exclaimed Thomas.

"It had something to do with what I said to Aunt May at tea. I thought I would mention that we had been looking at Albert's map to see what reaction I got from Charles. You should have seen his face, he couldn't hide his shock! I think he's trying to stop us snooping around the buildings on Aunt May's land. Mark my words Thomas, Charles is up to something and we need to find out what!"

Victoria the maid had run baths for Thomas and Catherine and put their pyjamas and nighty out ready for bed. Charles had brought up some coco and biscuits for the children then the butler and maid had bided them goodnight. As they sat drinking their coco and discussing the day's events and trying to decide their next move, it became apparent that their journey to the old barn had tired them out more than they had realised. So they both decided to call it a night and retire to bed.

Catherine was just drifting off into a deep sleep when she was awoken by a banging of a door, startled she jumped out of bed and went to the window to investigate. She could just make out Charles not in his butlers uniform but his own clothes, making his way with the help of a torch to the back garden gate.
"Where is he going at this hour?" she whispered to herself.

She threw on her dressing gown and wellington boots, picked up her own torch and quietly left her bedroom in the direction of Thomas' room. She softly tapped on his door and entered. Thomas was still fast asleep, so Catherine tip toed over to him and gave him a nudge.

Yawning he said angrily "What is it sis, I was asleep!"
"Shh, I've just seen Charles leave the house heading towards the woods. Quick get your dressing gown and wellington boots on, there's no time to get changed if we want to catch him up and find out where he's going!" replied Catherine as she made for the door.

They quickly and as quietly as possible made their way down to the kitchen door. Then outside and across the garden to the back gate, it was unlocked and ajar so they went through. Up ahead the children could just make out Charles' torch beam. They eventually caught up to Charles but not too close that they could give away their presence. Catherine turned off her torch and they both followed carefully in silence.

Charles clearly wasn't comfortable out in the woods at night. With every sound he heard he would frantically point his torch in that direction trying to see what was there, but to be relieved to find it was nothing.

After a while Thomas and Catherine realised that Charles was going in the same direction as they had earlier in the day. But when he got to the dried up stream, rather than cross it as the children had, he instead turned left and followed its bank further upstream. Charles eventually got to an old wooden bridge that spanned the stream; it didn't look like it had been used for some time as ivy had grown all over it.

Before crossing the bridge he quickly checked he wasn't being followed, shining his torch In an arc behind him. Thomas and Catherine had to take cover behind a fallen tree. When they peered up over the log, Charles was already over the wooden bridge and now following the opposite bank further upstream. So they leaped up and made their way over the bridge as well.

It wasn't long before Charles stopped in a small clearing, he rummaged around in a satchel he had on his shoulder. As he did the children thought it would be a good idea to take cover again, just in case. As they did the silhouettes of two men appeared out of the bushes and approached Charles, guns aimed at him. An exchange of words took place between the men, but the children were too far away to hear properly. Charles produced an envelope and gave it to one of the men. He lowered his gun and looked inside the envelope as Charles spoke to him. The man laughed out loud then he stepped closer to Charles, put a hand on his shoulder and as he spoke to him he gave him back the envelope. The two men then stepped away and retreated back into the darkness of the woods.

Charles stood there alone for a moment, reflecting on the encounter with the men. He returned the envelope to his satchel took a deep breath then turned to return home. Thomas and Catherine decided it would be a good idea to get home before him. In their haste the children made the decision to deviate off the path slightly to save time, they climbed over an old wooden fence and into an over grown field. They weaved around thorn bushes and small trees, stopping occasionally to check their direction back to the house. As the children raced on they came to a small clearing with the remains of a wooden structure. Two large wooden posts still jutted up out of the ground, pieces of timber lay scattered around them, almost as if they were covering something. It was difficult to see in the dark, even with the light of the moon which occasionally broke through the cloud cover. So they had to use their torches sparingly so as not to attract the attention of the approaching Charles.

When they got closer and shone their torches at the structure, they realised it was the remains of an old now disused well. Thomas moved closer and gingerly put his right foot on one of the wooden boards that lay across the top of the well.

"Looks pretty sturdy to me Catherine, let's edge across here and get through that bush" Thomas said pointing towards a sorry looking bush with a big hole in the middle of it, most likely made by a curious farm animal.

"I don't know about this Thomas, why don't we back track and find a different route, those boards look a bit rotten to me!"

"They'll be fine and besides, back tracking now would take too long and let Charles get in front of us. Then what would we do?"

Catherine thought for a moment then realised her brother was right and reluctantly agreed to carry on. Thomas smiled at his sister and held an out stretched arm towards her.

"Come on; hold my hand and I'll lead the way across"

Together they slowly edged their way across the wooden boards, which began to bend slightly and creak under the children's weight. Just as

Catherine was about to tell Thomas she had changed her mind, there was an almighty crack as the board beneath her feet gave way and broke into two pieces. She shrieked in panic as she began to fall through the newly formed hole. Thomas was caught completely by surprise and had to let go of his sister's hand and dive to safety. Meanwhile Catherine had fallen down to her waist; luckily her quick thinking had prevented her from falling completely through the hole. She had managed to stick out her arms at the last minute and now leant on her elbows. Thomas acted quickly and found the old, now rusty metal chain which was once attached to the wells bucket. He threw it over the metal bar which hung between the two upright posts and fished it down in front of Catherine.

"This better work!" he whispered to himself.

"Catherine grab hold of the chain, I can pull you up!"

Her instinct was to stay frozen to the spot, but she knew the boards which held her up could also give way at any moment. She took a deep breath and leant all her body weight onto one elbow, while grabbing hold of the dangling chain in front of her. Then transferring her weight onto the chain, she quickly grabbed it with her remaining hand. The rusty chains hoops snapped tight under Catherine's weight. The torch was on and lay on the ground pointing in her direction, dropped by Thomas when he dived to safety. The beam of light shone across the well and as Catherine slowly swung there in mid-air, she looked down to see the blackness below her feet. She could hear the occasional splash of stones from the well wall that had been dislodged by the fallen wooden boards.

"Quick Thomas, get me out of here before I lose my grip!" shrieked Catherine.

Her brother pulled on the rusty chain with all his mite, slowly the chain began to screech as it slid over the metal bar. With every heave of the chain, Thomas managed to pull his sister a little higher until she was completely out of the well.

He wrapped the end of the chain a few times around a nearby rock, which was enough to hold Catherine's weight and keep her suspended above the dark hole. He ran over to the edge of the well, held onto one of the posts with one arm then lent out and grabbed hold of Catherine's belt. He pulled with all his strength and she slowly began to swing back and forth until she cleared the well. At that moment she let go of the chain and fell to the safety of the floor, knocking her brother to the ground as well!

"Phew, that was way too close!" panted Thomas as he lay on his back.

Catherine nodded in agreement "Remind me never to agree to your crazy ideas again!"

Once she had given herself the quick once over to check she wasn't injured, she turned to Thomas,

"We'd better get our skates on if we're to make it back home before Charles now!"

In the mayhem that had occurred, Thomas had dived to the safety of the other side of the well then pulled Catherine over too.

"Quick through here, let's get going" shouted Thomas.

The children made their way through the sorry looking bush they had spotted earlier, which lead to a track that snaked off through the over grown field in the direction of the house. When they arrived, Thomas ran up to the kitchen door and turned the handle. The door was locked!

"Oh no we're too late; Charles has got back before us and locked it. Now what are we going to do?"

"I'm sure Sylvia keeps a spare key hidden somewhere over here!" Catherine whispered, pointing under the kitchen window. The children searched with their torches until they found a small loose brick, which was the likely hiding place. Thomas removed it and Catherine fished inside and pulled out the spare key.

Once the kitchen door had been unlocked and opened, the spare key was returned to its hiding place behind the loose brick. They entered the kitchen and quietly closed the door behind them. Thomas glanced up at the clock which hung on the wall, it read eleven thirty; he sighed and started to make his way out of the kitchen with Catherine following. She suddenly stopped and grabbed her brother by the shoulder.

"Hold on, we need to relock the kitchen door or Charles will know we have followed him out!"

"Thank goodness you remembered that!" Thomas whispered.

He ran over and relocked it, hanging the key back on its hook. Finally they made their way to Catherine's bedroom. The children discussed what they had just witnessed.

"Well now we know where the burglars are hiding out. I just can't believe Charles is a part of it all!" said Thomas

"He must have been supplying the burglars with details of the un-occupied mansions they could burgle. He must know staff from other properties in the area. I bet he strikes up a conversation with them in the village and they unknowingly tell him their owners are 'out of town' then he passes on the information" replied Catherine.

"You're probably right. Did you see one of the men pat Charles on the shoulder, must have been congratulating him on a job well done and telling him it was time to get his things together, ready for a quick getaway!"

"We need to tell Constable Finney before the three of them disappear. I think for now we just act normal around Charles so he doesn't get suspicious, agreed?" said Catherine. Thomas nodded in agreement.

"Right, you'd better get yourself in to bed quick sharp. We'll go to the police in the morning."

"Alright sis, see you in the morning"

With that Thomas left Catherine's room closing her door behind him.

Chapter 12

An owl hooted away in a nearby oak tree as the fog rolled in off the sea, heading towards Ashbourne House. A mixture of the dark night and fog made it almost impossible to see more than a few metres. Two dark figures slowly made their way across the garden towards the back of the house. Every few metres they would stop and crouch down to look and listen, checking the coast was clear, as they had done many times on previous burglaries. From where they were they could just make out the back door and kitchen window, no lights were on and it didn't look like anyone was up and about. John turned to Sid, "Go and check the back door, see if it's unlocked". As ordered Sid crept over to the door while John kept a look out. Slowly and as quietly as possible Sid tried the door handle. It squeaked a little but wouldn't open. So he crept back to John. "No luck mate, it's locked" he whispered.

"Right then we'll move onto the side of the house and try the next door. It doesn't look like anyone's up so I might as well use the torch to help us see a bit better in this damn fog!"

The two men picked up their holdalls and moved to the side of the house. Before getting to the side door they had to pass through the big iron garden gate. The gate was pad locked, as were all the gates on the estate. It was up to Albert as gardener to go around the estate before sunset and 'lock up', so it was secure for the night. After finding the candle stick in the field Aunt May had made him double check all doors, windows and gates on the estate.

Sid opened up his holdall and pulled out some bolt cutters, these made easy work of the pad lock. John removed the pad lock and threw it to one side with a thud. He then slid open the bolt and slowly opened the big iron gate with a loud screech of metal on metal, the two men cursed the noise as they passed through it.

Over in the garden shed, Albert was awoken by the screeching gate. He often slept in his shed after a long day's work, when he was too tired to cycle home to his nearby cottage. The shed was more than big enough to accommodate a bed and cupboard in one corner, Sylvia would always make him breakfast and a pot of tea the next morning.

As Albert had locked all the gates earlier that evening he knew something wasn't quite right. He got dressed, put on his boots and picked up a torch and his shotgun that were hung up near the door and headed outside to investigate.

John crept up the steps to the side door, put his holdall down on the floor and rooted around for some tools. He turned to Sid and whispered "go to the front of the house and check the front door and windows, see if there's an easier way in just in case I can't pick this lock!" Sid nodded and scurried off, carrying his holdall over his shoulder. John turned back to the door and went to work trying to pick the lock.

Albert took his time as he walked towards the garden gate. He knew that from his shed to the gate lay flower beds and part of the vegetable patch. It was dark and foggy and it could be potentially like a mine field. One wrong step and he could be falling into his beloved rose bushes or tripping over his prize winning marrows! He was a few metres from the gate when he stopped, crouched down and put his shotgun on the floor beside him. He turned off his torch and stuffed it into the belt of his trousers. He had heard a noise in the direction of the side of the house. He picked up his shotgun and edged forward through the gate towards the side door. As he got closer, Albert could see the silhouette of someone crouching in front of the side door. He moved a few steps closer while raising the shotgun; he then cocked it ready and aimed at the dark figure in front of him.

"Don't move Sonny!" shouted Albert. The dark figure froze, motionless in front of him.

"Now slowly stand up and back down the steps towards the sound of my voice" he ordered.

"It doesn't take a genius to bet you're the bloke

who's done all those burglaries. I think the police would love to have a little chat with you".

Suddenly Albert felt a hard thud on the back of his head and he screamed out in pain. As he fell to the floor he let go of the shotgun and as it crashed to the ground, it went off with a loud bang and the flash lit up the surrounding area. Albert managed to turn onto his back to see Sid stood over him, crowbar in his hand and a partially toothless grin on his face, then all went black.

With Albert taken care of, John turned to Sid and shouted "Get your things and let's get going the whole house will have heard that damn gun go off. It's only a matter of time before someone comes to investigate!" With that they ran back through the garden gate and off into the fields.

Thomas had woken suddenly to the shotgun blast. He'd got out of bed, put on his dressing gown and slippers and gone to the window to see if he could see anything. The children's bedrooms were situated at the back of the house overlooking the garden and fields. As he looked out there was a sudden break in the fog and it revealed the two men running from the scene, one turned to look back at the house and spotted Thomas at the window. Then they suddenly disappeared again into the foggy night.

Thomas met Catherine outside her bedroom.
"Crikey what's happened now, it feels like I'd only just nodded off!" said Catherine.
"I think I've just seen the same two men we saw Charles meet up with earlier in the evening. They were running away from the house, back into the woods!" replied Thomas.
"Well that doesn't sound good at all, come on let's go and see what's going on!"

They ran down stairs and out of the side door into the cold night air. Everyone from the household was already there, even Aunt May. Albert was just coming round; Charles was helping him to his unsteady feet. A shocked Aunt May told everyone to go inside to the study just in case the men were still lurking near the house. On the way in Charles turned to Victoria the maid and said "Victoria, go to the kitchen and get a cloth and some ice". Charles helped Albert into the study with everybody following. He sat him down in one of the big leather armchairs. Aunt May came over with a large glass of Brandy. "Here you go Albert drink this, I think you'll need it". Victoria came into the study; she placed a cloth filled with ice onto Albert's lump on the back of his head. He groaned in pain and said "I'm gonna have one heck of a headache in the morning!"

Charles asked him what had happened, so Albert explained to everyone, right up to him passing out after being hit over the head. Charles replied "As I came to your assistance Albert, I could just make out two figures running away".
"Did you see their faces?" enquired Aunt May.
"I'm afraid not ma'am, it was just too dark and foggy" replied Charles. Thomas interrupted "I saw them run off into the night. One of them looked back at the house and saw me watching. I

didn't see his face clearly as he had put shoe polish or something similar on it probably to blend into the darkness!"

"You'll have to be careful Thomas, these are dangerous men. If they know you saw them......" Charles paused for a moment,

"Well who knows what they're capable of, just look at what they did to Albert!" Aunt May intervened "First thing in the morning Charles can take Albert in the Bentley to the hospital, to have that nasty bump on his head checked. Thomas and Catherine can cycle into Abersoch and tell Constable Finney what's happened, you can ask him to come to the house. Victoria, can you make a spare bed up for Albert. You can stay here tonight. Right I think everyone should retire back to bed, it will be daylight soon". Everyone agreed.

Chapter 13

"One of those damn kids saw me!" hissed John. "What are we going to do, we'll have to take care of them then leave here later tonight. We can't have them giving a description of us to the old bill!" said Sid. "We'll go into Abersoch first thing and steal a van that can hold all our crates of loot. We'll get back to the hide out and load up the van, then make a call to our mate and arrange for the boat to pick us up tonight as soon as it's dark. I'll tell him to pick us up off the main beach cos we can drive straight onto there!" replied John.

Charles and a groggy Albert had driven to hospital earlier that morning in the Bentley. Aunt May and the rest of the staff carried on with their jobs and duties, until Constable Finney arrived hopefully later that morning.

Once Catherine and Thomas had finished a quick breakfast, they got their bikes, raced down the driveway and turned right onto the main road in the direction of Abersoch.

They peddled as fast as they could towards the town. Part of the way was downhill which was great, but they both knew it would be hard work peddling back up it later. They would both complain to each other about how difficult it was and probably get off their bikes and push them to the top of the hill! But that wasn't important right now; they would have to deal with that later. Their priority was to speak with Constable Finney as soon as possible.

It didn't take the children long to get to the police station in the middle of town. They screeched up outside the front doors, abandoning their bikes on the pavement and ran inside. Constable Finney and the young Constable Jones were just finishing their cups of tea and last night's paperwork, when the children burst in through the doors and ran up to the front desk.

"Ah you two again, I haven't got any more news on the stolen property you found. I have circulated a description of the two men to the local shop owners. So tell your aunt everything is being done and I will be in touch when I have more information" sighed Constable Finney. They explained to the two policemen exactly what had happened in the early hours of the morning. Constable Finney looked a little embarrassed "I am sorry for jumping the gun children; this could just be the lead we were after Constable Jones! Alright you two, go back home and tell your aunt that I'll come over to the house later this morning. I'll take a statement from Albert, Thomas you can give me a description of the man you saw as well. Do you think it is the same men who chased you from the cave?"

Thomas shrugged "yes I think so"

"I'll also have a look around the grounds to see if they have left any clues. O.k. thank you children, you better be getting back" said Constable Finney.

The children left the policemen to it, retrieved their bikes and began the tiring journey back to the hill and onwards to home.

They huffed and puffed as they pushed their bikes to the top of the hill.

"I'm shattered, let's have five minutes over there on that wall" said Thomas breathing heavily.

"Oh alright, but only five minutes as we need to get back and tell Aunt May when Constable Finney is coming" replied Catherine. So they lent their bikes against the wall and sat on top of it, catching their breath. Suddenly a vehicle came up the hill, screeching around the corner at speed, swerving towards Thomas and Catherine. "Watch out!" screamed Catherine as she jumped off the wall and into the safety of the field on the other side. "Ahh!" shouted Thomas as he fell backwards over the wall, just as the van mounted the grass verge and smashed into their bikes. They were sent flying into the air and crashed onto the road. The side of the vehicle slammed into the wall, sending fragments of stone and sparks flying everywhere. The driver didn't stop; they regained control of the van, veered off the grass verge and back onto the road and disappeared off in the direction of Pwllheli.

"Are you o.k. Thomas?" screamed Catherine as she ran to him.
"Ouch!! Yeah I'm alright I think. Just a few scratches from the wall and some damn nettle stings, they hurt the most! I need to find a dot leaf to rub on them"

Catherine could see that her brother was trying to laugh off what had just happened, but Thomas looked pale like he had seen a ghost! It had clearly shaken him up, her too she admitted to herself.

The children realised how lucky they had been, when they peered over the wall to see their mangled bikes in a heap in the middle of the road. "Who was that mad man, he could have killed us! They clearly can't drive can they!" said Thomas angrily.
"Don't think we can ride them home, look at the state of them, the wheels are all bent! Come on, we'd better go and get them off the road to a safe place" said Catherine.

Just as the children were trying to drag the bikes from the middle of the road the No.11 bus to Pwllheli appeared from around the corner. The bus pulled to the side of the road, the driver and the conductor got out and helped the children and their broken bikes onto the bus. They were dropped off at the entrance to Ashbourne House.
"Let's leave the bikes here; I'm not dragging it all the way to the house. Hopefully Albert can help us bring them back later, when he gets back from hospital" said Thomas.

The children trudged up the drive way, Thomas was limping slightly due to the scrapes on his legs.
"Did you see who was driving that van?" Thomas asked.

"No but it has to be those burglar's, don't forget you saw one of them last night and he'll be worried you could identify them both. I think that's why they were deliberately trying to run us over! One thing I did get was the van registration VHR227, I bet it's stolen!" replied Catherine.

"Well make sure you pass it onto Constable Finney when he arrives later" added Thomas.

When the children finally got back to the house they went straight to Aunt May to tell her what had happened. She was shocked but relieved they were alright. Victoria put some antiseptic onto Thomas' grazes, he yelped out in pain. At that moment Charles and Albert returned from the hospital, they rushed into the kitchen when they heard Thomas shout out.
"What happened to you then Tom, we saw your bikes at the main gates?" said Albert. When he learnt of their close shave, he replied angrily "Make sure you tell the police about this. These burglars are mad men and need to be stopped, they could have killed you" Charles looked both shocked and distracted, but agreed with Albert.

Later that afternoon the children decided enough was enough, they were going to confront Charles with all the information they had on him and his gang. They were going to give him the opportunity to tell Aunt May before the police were called. Thomas and Catherine asked Sylvia the cook if she knew where he was.

"Yes children, Charles asked your aunt if he could be excused from duty this afternoon as he was feeling unwell!" she said.

"Oh alright Sylvia, thanks" replied Catherine.

As they both left the kitchen, Thomas turned to Catherine "Do you think he knows we are onto him and he's done a runner?"

"I don't know, maybe. We can let the police know when they arrive!" she replied.

Chapter 14

Catherine and Thomas sat on the steps of Ashbourne House waiting for Constable Finney to arrive. Thomas fidgeted as he sat there, every few minutes he gave out a painful sigh as he found another ache or pain.

Eventually they could hear a vehicle approaching up the driveway. Constable Finney's police car appeared in the distance. It pulled up next to Catherine, Thomas and the front doors.

As Constable Finney exited his police car, he caught sight of a cut and bruised Thomas. "Oh dear looks like you've been in the wars today sonny!"

Before Thomas could reply, Aunt May appeared at the front door.
"Ah constable you're here, Please follow me to the dining room where we can talk"

So Constable Finney, Thomas and Catherine all followed Aunt May to the dining room. As they arrived at the door Aunt May directed Constable Finney in with an out stretched arm.

"Unfortunately my butler has been taken ill so we are a little disorganised today constable. Children can you get Victoria to bring some tea and fetch Albert from the garden please. I'm sure he needs to speak with the constable" she said.

"Alright Aunt May" replied Catherine as they both left the room.

"While we wait for my gardener and the refreshments, I would like to bring something more serious to your attention that happened this morning. On the way back from informing you of our attempted break in and assault of Albert Evans my gardener, my niece and nephew were nearly knocked down by a very reckless driver. Only their quick reactions saved them from certain injury!" Aunt May said to the constable.

"I noticed the young lad's cuts and bruises when I arrived. Well this is a very serious incident, so I'll need to find out exactly what happened" replied Constable Finney.

Just then Thomas and Catherine returned to the dining room. The constable turned to them "Your aunt informs me someone tried to knock you off your bikes this morning. Can you tell me what happened?"

He removed his note pad and pencil from his uniform breast pocket. The children went about telling him what happened and Catherine gave him the van's registration. "Mmm, if I'm not mistaken Constable Jones was taking some details of a van stolen from neighbouring Aberdaron as I was leaving the station. I will be able to confirm this when I get back to the station. It would appear that the burglars are becoming increasingly desperate and dangerous. They must think that you two can identify them from the chase at the cave or the attempted break in at Ashbourne house" replied the constable.

There was a knock on the drawing room door; Victoria entered carrying a silver tray with a pot of tea, biscuits and two glasses of lemon squash.

Albert followed in behind her removing his cap as he did so. He then proceeded to nervously fidget with it as he stood there. Victoria poured the tea for the three adults and gave the lemon squash to Catherine and Thomas, then left the room.

"Right Mr Evans can you tell me everything you remember about the events of early this morning, up to you getting knocked unconscious" asked Constable Finney. The constable wrote quickly as Albert told him what had happened. He paused occasionally to question Albert further and have a drink of his tea.

Once he was finished Constable Finney put his notepad and pencil back into his breast pocket and got to his feet.
"Lady Ripley the incident with the children will take priority, but I will keep you informed with both matters. Now children, I don't want you to worry, we'll find these men! Now if you'll excuse me, I need to carry on with my enquiries. Good day to you all, I'll see myself out" he said. With that the constable left the room.

Chapter 15

"Here Sid turn right mate!" directed John. The van turned off the main road into the beach car park and slowly drove up to the beach gate. It was early morning and the two men had come to check out the rendezvous point for the boat pick up later that evening. Once they were happy that no one was around, John got out of the van and walked around to the rear to get something out of his holdall. He re-appeared with the bolt cutters and went over to the gate. He cut the lock off with a 'Clunk' and it dropped to the floor, then he opened the metal gate so Sid could drive through onto the beach. Once through, John shut the gate again and got back into the van.
"Right, drive over there Sid and park up" he ordered. Sid drove over to a large sand dune, parked up and switched off the engine. The two men got out of the van and walked around to the front of it. John pulled a map out of his jacket pocket and began to open it. It was quite windy so he asked Sid to hold onto one end of the map, they then laid it on the van bonnet. John pointed

to a circle on the map "Right at 7.30 tonight, the boat is picking us up from here. Now by my estimations that is right where we are now. We can use this big sand dune as a marker for tonight."

"Will the boat crew help us get the loot on board?" enquired Sid.

"Yeah a couple of the crew will come ashore in a dingy as the boat will have to anchor a few hundred metres from shore, the quicker we get the loot and ourselves on the boat, the quicker we can get going! Right I've seen enough, we've got twelve hours to kill then we're home free" said John grinning.

The two men got back into the van; it started up and drove off back to the gate. John got out again and opened it up for Sid, when he closed it he put the cut pad lock back on so it looked as if the gate had never been opened! John had one last look around to make sure they hadn't been seen, he could see the wind and swirling sand were doing a nice job of covering up the tyre tracks on the beach. So he got back into the van and the two men drove off back to their hide out. They had to prepare for later. The loot had to be loaded into the van, the hide out had to be cleaned so it looked as if no one had been there, plus they had to check and clean their weapons and make sure they worked properly for tonight, just in case!

Un-be known to the two men they had been seen! Jack Stevens, the lighthouse keeper over at Warren Point had been doing his daily morning round. He'd been checking the large bulb and relevant machinery up at the top of the lighthouse when, out of the corner of his eye he spotted the blue van. Knowing that vehicles were prohibited from being on the beach, apart from the coastguard and he knew it wasn't there's! His curiosity got the better of him so he thought he'd take a closer look and grabbed his binoculars to see what they were up to. Jack took a description of the two men and the van's registration, make and model. He watched them until they left the beach and drove off out of sight, then he made his way back down the lighthouse stairs to his office to make a call.

"Hello Constable Finney it's Jack Stevens from the lighthouse"......
"I'm not too bad thanks"......
"Yeah the family is fine."
"Listen Bill it may be something and nothing, but after all these burglaries I keep reading about, I thought I should mention it!" said Jack.

He explained to Constable Finney what he had seen plus the descriptions of the men and the van details.
"They were heading back towards town no more than ten minutes ago."
"Ok Bill, glad it's of some use"
"Anytime"
"Goodbye Bill"

With that Jack put the telephone down, then got back to his duties.

Chapter 16

The children had asked Albert if he would help them bring their bikes back to the house, as they were still abandoned on the grass verge behind the main gate! He promised he would do it after tea as he had a lot of work to catch up on, having spent most of yesterday at the hospital or giving a statement to the police!

So Catherine and Thomas spent the day playing around the grounds of Ashbourne House. Aunt May had told them not to venture too far after everything that had happened.

It was early evening before they met Albert at his shed and the three of them headed off down the sweeping driveway to the main gates to retrieve their bikes. When they got to them, Albert surveyed the damage to the children's bikes. He huffed, puffed and tutted then said "well they've had a good old wallop haven't they!! I should be able to fix them for you, but I will have to get some new parts from Jones' bike shop in Pwllheli".

As Albert was working out if he could carry both the bikes back in one trip or would have to do two, a vehicle could be heard coming up the road from the town at speed. They all looked up as they could hear the high pitch revving of the engine and the screech of the tyres on the tarmac. A blue van sped past the main gates, heading in the direction of Pwllheli.
"Maniac!!" shouted Albert as he shook his fist at the van. Catherine and Thomas saw the van and looked at each other in surprise. Before either one could say anything a police car came speeding around the corner but braked hard and came to a stop outside the main gates. Constable Finney got out and came running over.

"Are you chasing that van Constable Finney?" asked Thomas eagerly.
"I've not much time, I need all three of you to come with me please, I will explain more in the car" replied Constable Finney.

Constable Jones was patiently waiting in the passenger seat for everyone to get into the police car. Albert, Catherine and Thomas got into the back through the driver's side, and then Constable Finney got in. He put the car into gear and stamped on the accelerator, the engine roared, the front wheels spun on the road and the car shot off.

"What's this all about constable?" demanded Albert.

"I think you probably saw a vehicle speed past you a few minutes before us. We have been following it since late this afternoon after receiving a tip off. We believe the occupants in the van are the burglars and the ones who tried to knock Catherine and Thomas over and tried to burgle Ashbourne House" replied the constable.

"Have you chased them from the old hunting lodge?" asked Thomas.

"We went to have a look at it this afternoon. We found that the dirt track leading to the building had been recently used as there were fresh tyre tracks! We parked at the end of the track and found the hunting lodge on the other side of a small wood. The front door had been forced open; when we entered we found two camp beds and food. The old fire place had been used as well; it looked like it had been used for some time. It was the perfect hideout, quiet and off the beaten track!" said Constable Finney.

"So how did you end up chasing the burglars?" asked Catherine.

"We had a look around then headed back to the police car. As we were getting ready to leave, a van turned onto the dirt track, spotted us and skidded to a stop. They then reversed back on to the road at speed and screeched off. So we decided to give chase, presuming it was the burglars. For the last hour we have been in pursuit of the van all around the peninsula as they tried to give us the slip!" replied Constable Finney.

Then Constable Jones turned around and said smugly "We backed off enough to let them think they had lost us because we knew where they were heading anyway. We believe they are trying to make a run for it. We had a tip off of a possible rendezvous point and a fishing boat which will be anchored in the bay. We think this evening the rest of the gang will come closer to shore to pick them up."

"We'll be there to arrest them all" replied Constable Finney.

"But how are you two going to arrest the burglar's and all the boat crew?" asked Thomas.

"Good question young man. We have officers from the Pwllheli police assisting us tonight. Also the coast guard are anchored in the next bay just in case the fishing boat tries to make a run for it, they can intercept them" said Constable Finney.

"So why did you want us to come with you? It sounds like you have this situation all sewn up!" exclaimed Albert.

"You have all had a glimpse of one or both of the burglars so you will be taking a look at them for me, to make a positive identification before we go in and arrest them. Don't worry this will be done from a distance" replied Constable Finney.

The police car eventually reached the beach car park and slowed down as it made the turn in to it. As they entered the parking area, the red lights of the men's van could just be seen in the distance driving through the gate onto the beach. Constable Finney had already turned off his head lights, just in case the two men were checking behind them to make sure they weren't being tailed. The police car made a left turn and slowly crawled over to the far corner of the car park out of sight and stopped.

The police constable turned off the car's engine and the five of them sat in silence. Constable Finney turned to Constable Jones and said "Alright Jones, check everyone is here". With that Constable Jones got out of the car and walked ahead a few metres. He then got out his torch and flashed it on and off three times in the direction of some sand dunes. Instantly he got three flashes back from the sand dunes, then slowly black silhouettes came into view. Six figures crept up to the police car as Constable Finney, Albert and the children got out.

Sargent Ivor Thomas walked over to Constable Finney and in a low voice said "Evening Bill, just seen the van drive onto the beach making its way to the rendezvous point. I've spoken to the coast guard on the radio; they're in position and awaiting further instructions.

Now this is your operation Bill, it's on your patch so where do you want us lot?"
"Thanks for your help Sarge! If we all fan out along the sand dunes behind the rendezvous point. The children and Albert here are going to take a look at them and hopefully give us a positive I.D. Then when they start loading the loot onto the fishing boat, we've got them caught in the act. I'll then give the signal for us to swing into action. Do you have your portable search light and weapons?" said Constable Finney.
"Yes Bill, we have the light plus two pistols and a rifle. Myself and you Bill, will take the pistols and one of my men will have the rifle, alright?" replied Sargent Thomas.
"Right on my signal, Constable Jones will have our portable search light and he'll be at one end

of the sand dune pointing it at the van, if you can have one of your men at the other end of the sand dune pointing your portable search light at the fishing boat. That will cover the area we need.

"Tell your men to keep out of sight behind the dunes, we don't know if these me are armed. We know they are dangerous and could use force. Right, I think that covers everything. Let me know when you're all in position Sarge!" said Constable Finney.
"Will do Bill" replied Sargent Thomas and he turned and headed to his Constables to give the orders out.

Eventually everyone kept low and quietly made their way over to the sand dunes.

Chapter 17

Albert, Thomas and Catherine had followed Constable Finney over to the sand dunes behind the burglars rendezvous point.

As everyone got into position, the children and Albert lay against the damp sand. It was now dark and the children could see the stars in the clear night sky. With the sun now gone, it was starting to get cold. The children could see their breath when they breathed out and they were starting to shiver, luckily Constable Finney had brought a blanket for the children to sit on, so they used that to wrap around them both. Constable Finney checked Sargent Thomas and his men were ready with the thumbs up sign, the Sargent looked around his men then gave the thumbs up back. Slowly and carefully Constable Finney crawled to the top of the sand dune and peered over the top. He scanned the beach through his binoculars to see what was happening. The van by now had reversed to the water's edge; the two men were at the rear already off-loading a large crate on to the sand in preparation for the fishing boats arrival.

Constable Finney ducked back down then one by one asked Catherine and Thomas to carefully take a quick look to positively identify the two men. One at a time the children took the binoculars and crawled up to the top of the dune with the Constable to take a look. They both told him that they were pretty sure it was the right men, so he then lay on top of the dune waiting for the fishing boat to arrive at the rendezvous point!

There was a deadly silence behind the sand dune as everyone looked nervously towards Constable Finney waiting for the signal to go! All that could be heard was the sea lapping at the shore and the two men heaving the crates from the back of the van onto the sand.

After what seemed like hours, Constable Finney heard it first, the dull drown of a chugging diesel engine. He scanned the sea and eventually spotted the outline of the fishing boat making its way towards the shore. The fishing boat had turned all its lights off, but he could see one of its crew flashing a torch towards the shore. He moved his gaze back to the van and could see one of the men flashing their torch at the fishing boat in reply. The boat captain saw it and adjusted his course slightly.

Constable Finney crawled over to Sargent Thomas and whispered "They're off-loading the stolen goods in crates and the boat's just turned up in the bay and making its way towards the shore."
"I reckon the fishing boat won't be able to get all the way in as the bay is quite shallow, so I expect some of the crew will have to come ashore to help." replied Sargent Thomas. "Right I'll keep observing until they start loading the crates onto the boat" said Constable Finney, and then he crawled back up to the brow of the sand dune to carry on observing.

As he looked on, sure enough as the Sargent had said, the fishing boat stopped about one hundred metres short of the shore and dropped anchor. The crew then got busy on deck preparing a dingy to be lowered over the side. The captain stayed on-board and sent two of his crew over the side down into the dinghy. They untied the tethering rope attached to the fishing boat and gentle floated away. Once clear, one of the men fired up the little two stroke outboard engine and the two men sped towards the shore.

John looked out towards the oncoming dingy "Here's the dinghy Sid and about time too. We need to get moving before someone spots us".

The dinghy slid onto the beach and the two crewmen jumped out. They went over to the first crate and picked it up then took it to the dinghy, heaving it in. One crewman turned and said to John "we can only take one crate at a time, how many of them are there?"
"There's three crates, and then us two, that's

four trips so you better get a move on mate" replied John angrily.

The four men then dragged the dinghy off the beach and back into the water, turning it around so it pointed back towards the fishing boat. John was just about to warn the crewmen that if they tried to double cross them and do a runner with the crate, he'd kill them all, when search lights suddenly light up the area of the van, dinghy and the four men.

"Damn it Sid, it's the police, we must have been followed. Quick take cover behind the van" ordered John.

"I hope you two have guns on you because this could turn nasty" Said Sid.

"Yeah we have pistols. I suggest you two cover us with gun fire and we'll get this crate to the boat, then come back for you two. We'll have to leave the other two crates. It's our only chance of getting away with something" suggested one of the crewmen.

"O.k. but you better come back for us!" warned John.

Chapter 18

Constable Finney had seen the first crate go onto the dinghy, so he'd given the signal and the operation had swung into action. Everyone except Thomas, Catherine and Albert, had made their way to the top of the dune. The two police constables at either end of the line of men had switched on their search lights and pointed them in the direction of the gang. Sargent Thomas and one of his constables were aiming their pistol and rifle at the four men, Constable Finney had drawn his pistol with one hand and had a loudhailer in the other. Before he spoke he shouted to Albert, Catherine and Thomas to keep down and stay there.

"This is the police, the games up lads; you are surrounded so I suggest you throw any weapons out from behind the van and one by one come out with your hands up!" ordered the Constable.

Suddenly from behind the van all hell broke loose, a hail of gun fire rang out. Some bullets hit the sand dune in front of the police with a thud sending sand flying into the air, some bullets could be heard whizzing overhead. But one hit the search light Constable Jones was holding with a loud bang, shattering the glass and sending shards of glass falling onto his head, it was his instinct to drop the broken search light and cover his head with his arms while diving back behind the sand dune. Everyone else took cover too, except the poor constable with the other search light who was ordered by Sargent Thomas to remain where he was.

As the fire fight broke out, Thomas and Catherine huddled close to Albert for protection, both of them covering their ears with their hands as the noise was deafening!

The police returned fire, peppering the van with bullet holes. Constable Finney tried once again to negotiate their surrender.
"This is your last chance, there is no escape.

Drop your weapons and come out with your hands up!"

More shots were fired at the police. At that point, Constable Finney could hear the dinghy's engine roar into life and he could see them fleeing to the waiting fishing boat. Within seconds they were alongside the vessel and climbing aboard. In their panic to get away, the men decided to abandon the loot and dinghy leaving them to float away in to the bay. Before he could shout to Sargent Thomas to radio the coastguard to stop the fishing boat, he could see them speeding in to the bay with their search light aimed on them. Then he heard them on their loudhailer.
"Fishing boat crew this is the coastguard, shut down your engines and drop your anchor immediately, you are under arrest".

The captain took no notice of the coastguard's demands; he pulled up his anchor, put the boats engine onto full power and started to make a sharp left turn away from the shore. The coastguard fired their big machine gun across the bow of the fishing boat, sending water dancing up in front of them. This was enough to change the captain's mind and he shut his engine down and dropped his anchor immediately. The coastguard drew up alongside the fishing boat and boarded it to arrest the crew.

Meanwhile John and Sid were oblivious to the fishing boat crew's fate, they were still busy shooting at the police, trying to hold them back and buying themselves time. But they were fast running out of bullets. The police were doing their best to pin them down behind the van by returning fire. All of a sudden John screamed out in pain and crumpled in a heap on the sand. Sid turned and crouched down beside him.
"Ahh, I'm hit Sid!"

When Sid looked down at John's leg he could see his trouser leg starting to turn red. So he took off his own belt and used it as a tourniquet to tie it around his wound and try to stem the blood flow. John was trying to get up so he could keep firing back at the police, but he was struggling to get to his feet. Sid realised that their situation was only going to get worse and there was no escape now. He turned to John "come on mate, we both know this is it. Your hit and bleeding badly and we're nearly out of bullets, this will end up with one or both of us dead and I'd rather go to prison than die for some jewellery". John looked up at Sid and nodded in agreement, then hissed through gritted teeth "you're right mate, but it ain't just us who'll be going down for this mark my words!"

Sid took John's gun and his own and threw them out from behind the van. He then began to help John to his feet; he got one of his arms around his neck so he could take some of his weight. They both then slowly made their way out from behind the van and towards the police with their free hands in the air.

Constable Finney had seen the guns thrown from behind the van and ordered everyone to cease firing, but to still aim their guns in the direction of the burglars, just in case it was a trick!

"Don't shoot we're surrendering, look there are our guns" shouted Sid.
"Take ten paces forward, then lie face down on the sand" ordered Constable Finney through his loudhailer.

The men did as they were told, then Constable Finney signalled to Sargent Thomas and his constables to move in and arrest them. They handcuffed the two men and lead them to a waiting police van. By now Constable Finney had made it to the arrested men.
"Just to let you know we've arrested the rest of your gang on the boat and retrieved all the stolen goods. You'll be going to prison for some time!" he said triumphantly. John turned to Constable Finney and replied smugly "well you haven't got the mastermind yet have you. He'll be someone familiar to you I expect, old Charlie boy the butler at Ashbourne House!"

As the two men passed Albert, Thomas and Catherine who were huddled together, they all stared at one another. John shouted to the children "We should've made sure we'd taken care of you this morning, shame we only ran over your bikes!"

Constable Finney grabbed him by the shoulder, "Well you've just implemented yourself into an attempted hit and run as well".
Sid barged into John with his shoulder and hissed "Shut up will you John we're in enough trouble as it is!"

Constable Finney had heard enough and ordered the two constables to take them away.

Chapter 19

Constable Finney wasn't sure if there was any truth to the burglar's statement about Charles the butler; his priority was to follow it up and speak to him as soon as possible. He walked over to where Albert, Catherine and Thomas were standing. "I'm sorry you had to be subjected to that and I must apologies for putting you in danger but we didn't know they were armed and ready to use them, plus it escalated quicker than anyone expected! This is the reason we tried to keep you out of the way when the gun shots started. Are you all alright, a bit shook up I expect?" he said.

"Yeah we're alright thanks, the kids are a little shaken but no harm done" replied Albert.

"It was kind of exciting, just like a cowboy film!" said Thomas.

"We knew you'd keep us safe and stop them Constable Finney" added Catherine.

"Good, as long as you are alright. I'll see if one of the constables has a flask of tea you can have, let's try and warm you up a bit eh!"

"One more thing, one of the arrested men is claiming that your aunt's butler Charles is the mastermind of all the burglaries and head of the gang. So I will need to come and speak to him straight away" said Constable Finney, he then walked away to go and sort out the tea's.

The children both looked at Albert, he looked astonished by the constable's statement.
"I don't believe any of that rubbish! I've known Charles for a long time. He can be a little strange sometimes but he's no criminal, there must be some other explanation" he replied.
"Well we followed him into the woods last night and he met up with the two men. It certainly looked like he knew them" said Thomas.
"Yeah and he gave them an envelope. We think he's been passing the rest of the gang information about which houses to burgle!" added Catherine. Albert just stood there with his hand rubbing his forehead,
"I just can't believe it! He must have been forced into helping them" he sighed.

"You might be right Albert, maybe they were blackmailing him for information?" said Thomas.

Constable Finney walked back over to Albert and the children.
"Come on you three, you can drink your tea in my car as I think we better get back and find your butler Charles quickly".

Chapter 20

The journey home was quiet, the two policemen were reflecting on a successful operation, Albert and the children were trying to take in everything that had happened and what they had just been told by Constable Finney.

Thomas turned and whispered to Catherine "I wonder why they are trying to blame Charles? They were the ones caught with the crates of 'loot'! Maybe it's a last ditched attempt to try and wriggle out of their crimes".
"Maybe! Or its possible Albert's right and he was forced into it. Well we'll find out soon enough, look we're home!" Catherine whispered back.

The two children looked out of the car window as they turned and began to make their way up the familiar sweeping driveway to Ashbourne House.

As the two policemen, Albert and the children were all getting out of the car, to their surprise Charles was already at the front door waiting.

"Ah Charles just the person I need to speak to, is there somewhere we can have a chat?" asked Constable Finney.
"Yes Constable there is, please follow me to the drawing room, Lady Ripley is awaiting your arrival" he replied.

Everyone followed Charles to the drawing room. As he got to the drawing room door, he knocked and then entered.
"Lady Ripley, Albert and the children have been brought back safely by the police. They are all outside" he announced.
"Thank you Charles, see them in please" replied Aunt May.

Charles turned to the policemen, Albert and the children and beckoned them into the drawing room with an out stretched arm. He then followed in behind them and closed the door.
"Lady Ripley I must apologies for taking your niece and nephew without your permission. But our operation to capture the burglars was fast moving and we had to act quickly to apprehend

them before they tried to escape. Albert and your niece and nephew were the only people to have seen them and could hopefully make a positive identification of the men before we moved in to arrest them" said Constable Finney.

"This would not have been acceptable under normal circumstances, but these were far from normal circumstances. Plus Albert had accompanied them so I accept your apology Constable" Replied Aunt May.

"We are here Lady Ripley because the two men arrested for the burglaries have made some serious accusations towards a member of your staff so we need to speak with them" asked Constable Finney.

"The person in question has already come to me and has confessed to what has been going on! Now before you question them I need to state for the record that they would have come forward sooner with the Information, but once they had confided in myself, the police were already on the tails of the burglars and the information was not important enough at the time to delay you any further! I just hope that now you have arrested the men, you will understand why there was a delay in contacting you" replied Aunt May. The two children looked at each other "So it is true Charles is the gangs leader!" said Thomas.

Then suddenly before anyone could say anymore, Charles cleared his throat and replied "Its true Constable Finney I have 'come clean' as you might phrase it! But the whole situation isn't as it appears or as the arrested man has stated. For one of the arrested men is my son John!"
"What!!" was the unified reply from Albert, Thomas and Catherine?
"I think I will need to explain from the beginning" exclaimed Charles.

Chapter 21

Everyone in the room apart from Aunt May had a look of shocked confusion, not quite believing what they were being told.

Charles sighed then took a deep breath and began to explain. "As most working class couples with a new born child, myself and my wife were no different and struggled to make ends meet.

We lived in a deprived part of the East end of London and as my son John became a young boy he began to get in with the wrong crowd as I wasn't around much to keep him in check! Mrs Bates did the best she could to discipline him as did I when I was home, but John got into more and more trouble.

I tried to balance fatherhood with work but found myself working longer and longer hours. I was fortunate enough to be offered a job in Brighton as the Family I worked for in London had a seaside retreat there, they needed a butler to run the property so I was offered the position. It was a great opportunity for us all. It was hoped that I would go first, then a month or two later my wife and son would follow me. Then maybe we could get John out of the trouble of his London life and give him a fresh start.

Unfortunately he was in a gang and participating in some petty criminal activities, but serious enough to see him arrested and sent to a prison for young juveniles.

This was the last straw for Mrs Bates; she never really recovered from the stress of bringing John up then him ending up in prison. I'm afraid the two of them never made it to Brighton to be with me.

My wife, tired and completely run down, contracted pneumonia and died a few weeks later. I was devastated and took leave and came back to London. I visited John in prison to break the terrible news to him and was shocked and upset that he barely showed any emotion or remorse towards his mother's death. It was at this point that I told him if that is how he felt then I no longer had a son and that my John had perished with my wife, his mother.

Family and friends paid their respect at the funeral. The Prison gave John permission to attend with a prison officer chained to him, but he refused. After the funeral I went back to Brighton but it was clear that I needed a fresh start as it was too hard for me to forget that we were so close to all being there as a family and turning over a new leaf in our lives.

The Donaldson's were kind enough to pass my credentials onto their friend Lady Ripley, who offered me a role as Butler here at Ashbourne House which I gratefully took.

I never spoke to my son once I moved to Wales. I received letters from my brother Bert; he kept me informed of what John was doing. Disappointingly he had slid further into the criminal world and was in and out of prison. I had asked my brother not to reveal to John my whereabouts if he ever asked.

So that was that, I got on with my life as best I could until about a months ago. I was running an errand for Lady Ripley; I bumped into Mrs Cynthia Davis who regularly attends Lady Ripley's coffee and reading mornings. She informed me that she had overheard two ruffians asking after me in Pwllheli's Post Office. Luckily the post master didn't tell them where I was as he thought they looked like trouble.

Then I started to read about all these burglaries and worryingly concluded that it must have been John and his gang. I didn't know how he found where I was, but I knew it was only a matter of time before he would find me as Abersoch is a small place.

Sure enough one afternoon about two weeks ago I was sweeping the front steps and checking the front of the house was tidy, when two men appeared from the fields nearby. I knew straight away it was John and he recognised me. He basically threatened me claiming his stays in prison were down to me not being there when he was a child, and that I 'owed him'. He asked if I'd heard about all the burglaries, grinning as he told me. He confessed to all of them and said that Ashbourne House was the last one on their list. He knew there were valuables and as butler I would have access to it all.

He tried to blackmail me into leaving a door unlocked one night when he chose, so they could gain entry. If I didn't people would get hurt. If I tried to go to the police he would plant some of the stolen valuables at Ashbourne House and send an anonymous letter informing them and claiming I was the mastermind to all the burglaries and head of a notorious gang and being a butler was all just a perfect front. Then I would witness first hand as he had the terror of time in prison!

This was when you two Thomas and Catherine, spotted me talking to John and his accomplice as you arrived back from the Market with your Aunt in the Bentley. I had refused to assist his gang with the burglary of Ashbourne House. I told him to just leave Abersoch and take what he had already stolen with him. I said I wouldn't say anything to anyone if he just left. Of course I had no intention of letting him get away with all those stolen goods. I would have told the police straight away. John refused and said he'd be back and that I should 'watch my back'. When I realised that he might have seen the children that morning as they returned from the market with Lady Ripley, I knew I had to act quickly. I didn't know what he might do to make me co-operate!

I went to the post office and drew out all my life savings. I was pretty sure that they were hiding out somewhere on Ashbourne house land, when Thomas and Catherine found the candlestick in nearby fields. I checked the map of the land which Albert had, to see what outbuildings there were. Then Catherine told Lady Ripley over diner that they had been out to look at an old barn, but it was derelict and falling down. I knew John and Sid must be hiding out in the old hunting lodge. Later that night I headed off over there to find them, I wanted to try and reason with them one last time. When I eventually found them or should I say they found me! I offered them an envelope with my life savings money in it. I asked them to take the money and leave that night and leave the stolen 'loot' in the hunting lodge. Then once they were gone I would make an anonymous call to the police tipping them off to the whereabouts of it. But he just laughed in my face saying it wasn't enough, plus they had worked damn hard to burgle all those properties and they weren't just going to give it up. Then he told me to get lost before I got hurt, so I had no choice but to leave them".

"Ahh that makes sense as we followed you because we thought you were up to something. When we saw you handing over that envelope we presumed it was information on more potential houses for them to burgle!" said Catherine.

"Goodness gracious children, I would never have done that. I was naive and stupid for doing what I did but I wouldn't have added assisting criminals to that!" replied Charles

"Things escalated quickly with the attempted break in at Ashbourne House then Thomas and Catherine being nearly knocked over. I had to take his threats seriously. I faked illness and asked to be excused from my duties so I could go back to the old hunting lodge and tell them that enough was enough, that they had gone way too far. I was going to tell them that I would tell the police where they were and that was the end of their rampage. But when I arrived there it was deserted, I was too late! So I came straight back and thought it best to inform Lady Ripley about everything. I just hope I didn't hamper your investigation and subsequent arrest of John and his gang Constable Finney? I didn't know the gangs whereabouts until last night when I tried to pay them off. I sincerely apologise and will accept any punishment necessary".

Constable Finney had been busy scribbling into his note pad taking a brief statement as Charles explained. It took him a few minutes before he was finished. He sighed to himself and rubbed his forehead then put his note pad away.

Then he addressed everyone present.
"In the light of what you have said tonight Charles, it appears to me that you were under incredible pressure by the gang to do as they ordered. The fact that you didn't is a great credit to you. Luckily no one was hurt as a result of you keeping this information from us, well except for the lump on Albert's head!

At the end of the day the gang was caught and arrested and the stolen items were retrieved so as far as I am concerned there was no harm done. But take this little talk as a dressing down, you should have come to the Police as soon as they first confronted you! Please make sure you don't withhold information like that again. Now if you will all excuse me it has been quite an eventful night and I need to get back to the station and interview the two men we have in custody. Charles you will need to come down to the station tomorrow afternoon to give a formal statement please".

With that Constable Finney left the room.

Chapter 22

Thomas and Catherine ran over to Charles and gave him a big hug.
"We knew something wasn't right about all this, we knew those two men were lying!" said Catherine.
"Thank you children, it means a great deal to me, I am just relieved that no one got hurt and that this is all over" replied a relieved Charles.

The children had had a long and exciting evening; it was late so they had been ordered to bed by Aunt May. Charles had brought up some warm milk and biscuits which they ate in Catherine's room.
"It's going to be a bit boring for the rest of the holidays, now this is all over!" Thomas sighed.
"It was exciting wasn't it Thomas. Can you imagine the look on mum and dad's faces when we tell them!"

They both chuckled to each other.

Thomas yawned and stretched then got up to leave the room; he turned to Catherine and said "I'm exhausted I'm off to bed. Night sis, see you in the morning"

"Good night, don't dream too much about tonight eh!" she replied grinning.

Chapter 23

A week later Catherine and Thomas' parents arrived at Ashbourne House to collect their children and take them back home to London. When Aunt May had told the children's parents about their holiday adventures they nearly had heart attacks. They had been reassured they were never in any danger and were in fact the ones that helped the police apprehend the burglars! Abersoch's local councillor Arthur Davis had given them both bravery awards in a ceremony that took place at the town hall. The Pwllheli Evening News had interviewed the children and taken pictures for the weekly edition. Aunt May had been so proud of the children she had the bravery awards framed for them, so they could hang them on their bedroom walls at home.

As a thank you to Aunt May for looking after Catherine and Thomas over the summer holidays, their parents treated them all to lunch at the Sandpiper restaurant in the village.

Aunt May said she would drive them all in the Bentley to the restaurant, but the children's dad decided he would drive as he knew all too well how bad his sister's driving was, and they wanted to get there in one piece. So they all hopped into the car and drove down to the village, they had to park a few minutes away from the restaurant. As they all walked down the high street to the restaurant, people kept stopping the family to speak to the children, saying comments like; "Well done you two" and "here are the two heroes!!" They were like local celebrities.

Thomas and Catherine beamed with pride, their dad ribbed them that their heads were growing so big that they might not get through the restaurant door!

Chapter 24

Before they knew it their holiday had finally come to an end. Albert and Charles had loaded up the Bentley with their suitcases and they both stood next to the car waiting for the family. Aunt May stood on the door step of Ashbourne House weeping; she hated saying goodbye to them all. She hugged Catherine and then Thomas tightly and said "I've really enjoyed you two being here, it's been a little more eventful than I was expecting! It will be quiet when you've gone. I just hope you have enjoyed your holiday here?"
"It's been fantastic Aunt May, the best holiday yet!" said Thomas.
"Wait until we tell our friends what we got up to, they will be really envious!" replied Catherine.

Aunt May then moved on to Thomas and Catherine's parents. "I hope you're not too angry Peter, Mary. I am sorry about the whole thing".

"That's alright May; there is nothing to be sorry about. Let's just be thankful that no one got hurt" replied their dad.

The children then ran over to Albert and hugged him.
"Now you two have a safe journey home alright. I'm gonna miss you both. I'll start counting the days until your next summer holidays, hopefully I will have fixed your bikes by then!" he said.
"Ah thanks Albert, we're going to miss you too!" replied Catherine.
"Don't get into any more trouble when we've gone, alright Albert" chipped in Thomas.

Albert laughed and patted both the children on the head, "You've got yourself a deal!"

They all said their goodbyes and got into the Bentley, Charles started it up and they slowly moved away. Aunt May stood at the door waving and the children waved back until they could no longer see her as the car dropped down the driveway to the main gates and out of view.

Catherine and Thomas both felt sad, the summer holidays had flown by due to the exciting adventure that had happened to them. They only had three more days left then it was back to school and another school year!

On the way to Pwllheli train station they passed the beach car park, the children pointed out to their parents that this was where the shoot out and subsequent arrests had taken place. Their mum and dad just looked at each other and shook their heads in disapproval.

Once at the train station, Charles parked the Bentley and helped the family carry their luggage to the platform. The station was quiet now as most of the holiday makers had already gone home.

Before leaving the family to return back to Ashbourne House, Charles asked Catherine and Thomas' dad if he could have a quiet word.
"Sir I would just like to take this opportunity to apologies for the situation I put Master Thomas

and Miss Catherine into. If I'd had any indication that they were in danger I would have moved quicker to contact the police. But as Lady Shipley explained to you, Threats were made towards myself and your family and I had to take those threats seriously."

"It's alright Charles. I know you were in a difficult position, I just wished you would have contacted the police a lot sooner. The situation could have been a lot more serious. But in the end the police got the gang and no one was hurt, so that is good." the children's dad replied.

Charles said goodbye to Catherine and Thomas' parents and then turned to the children.
"Master Thomas, Miss Catherine, you be good for your parents on the journey home. I'm sorry about everything that happened". Then he crouched down closer to the children and whispered with a smile "I hope it was a more exciting summer holiday for you both than usual!" and he winked at them. Catherine and Thomas smiled and both hugged him.

Charles left as the family boarded the train bound for London Euston. As they all settled into their carriage compartment, Thomas looked out of the window and excitedly "I can't wait until next summer holiday, who knows what adventures we could have?"

Their parents looked at one another, then their dad said "Well, your mother and I have been talking and we think it would be a good idea if you both came with us to the Red Cross mission in Africa next summer holidays. That way we can both keep an eye on you two. We will talk more about it when it gets closer to the time alright". The children both signed and agreed.

But then a grin appeared on Catherine's face and she turned to Thomas and whispered "Hey, imagine what an adventure that could be!" Thomas thought for a second then nodded and smiled back "Yeah good thinking sis, it could be our best one ever!"

THE END

Printed in Poland
by Amazon Fulfillment
Poland Sp. z o.o., Wrocław